Higslaff the Pawnshop Owner needs a job done, but the Guild War has taken a toll. Those he'd normally call upon are engaged in some other vital assignment, or dead.

He decides to hire Gurk, Jax, Marigold, Lysine and Kalgore instead. The adventuring party has proven themselves resourceful and effective on previous jobs, not only for himself, but for the local silversmith, and the Church of Apollo. This particular assignment shouldn't be a problem.

What Higslaff doesn't know is that details of his job have been compromised. Agents of the Riven Rock Thieves' Guild are on the move, ready to wrest control of the enchanted item that could tip the balance in the Guild War.

Praise for Monsters, Maces and Magic

"Ervin's imagination is fueled by Tolkien's sweat, Willy Wonka's blood, and Clint Eastwood's attitude. A crazy mix to be certain, but a combination that makes for amazing possibilities." Ray Johnson, LitRPG Audiobook Podcast

"Exciting and hilarious! It feels like a true game with friends." Dueling Ogres Podcast

"I was pulled into the world and could see the rules of the world unfold. This really does feel like a game. A fun game that I am going to have to continue." Casia's Corner

Pawn

Monsters, Maces and Magic

Terry W. Ervin II

Pawn- Monsters, Maces and Magic Book Five
Copyright © 2020 Terry W. Ervin II

All rights reserved. No portion of this book may be reproduced in any form without permission from the publisher, except as permitted by U.S. copyright law.

Published by Gryphonwood Press
www.gryphonwoodpress.com

Cover art by Mario Barraza
Edited by K.S. Brooks

This is a work of fiction. All characters are products of the author's imagination or are used fictitiously.

ISBN: 978-1-950920-15-0

BOOKS BY TERRY W. ERVIN II

Monsters, Maces and Magic
Outpost
Betrayal
Guild
Fairyed
Pawn
Date

Crax War Chronicles
Relic Tech
Relic Hunted
Relic Shield (forthcoming)

First Civilization's Legacy
Flank Hawk
Blood Sword
Soul Forge

Stand-Alone
Thunder Wells

Collections
Genre Shotgun

Dane Maddock Universe
Cavern

Dedication

This novel is dedicated to Eric Bowser, a co-worker who lost his battle to pancreatic cancer while I was completing Pawn. Eric was a caring and funny man, loving husband and father, and an innovative teacher and technology supervisor. He was a longtime supporter of my writing and shared many of my novels with his sons.

He is and will continue to be missed.

Acknowledgements

First, I would like to thank Kathy, my wife, and Genevieve and Mira, my daughters, for their patience and understanding. They allowed me the countless hours to imagine, plot, research, write, revise and edit—all things necessary to complete **Monsters, Maces and Magic: Pawn**.

Second, I would like to thank my family, friends, co-workers, and the members of *Flankers*, all of whom encouraged, questioned, and prodded me along to finish **Pawn**.

Third, I'd like to thank the folks at Gryphonwood Press, especially David Wood for not only believing enough in **Flank Hawk** (my first novel) to publish it, but for his continued insight and advice, and an avenue for me to reach readers, offering them the tales I want to share.

Fourth, I want to thank Mario Barraza for applying his artistic talent, practiced skill, and attention to detail in creating the cover art.

Fifth, Kendra Oldaker, for naming a character in the novel, Elisha Justine Woolwine. It was a pleasure to work with Kendra while discovering the added dimension the sentinel brought to the story. Kendra was selected from among the members of *Flankers* and the readers who receive my newsletter.

That leaves you, the reader. You are the primary reason I wrote **Monsters, Maces and Magic: Pawn**. Thank you for choosing my fantasy novel from the hundreds of thousands available. I truly hope you enjoy the tale. With that in mind, don't hesitate to post a review or send an email to let me know your thoughts. You can learn more about my works at www.ervin-author.com, along with a link to receive my newsletter.

Prologue

The barren drylands south of Three Hills City

Kyreen Shortcuff lay next to a gully under a moonlit sky, her body broken and sliced. Once again she lapsed beyond feeling physical pain. Twice the cleric had cast cure spells upon her, each time restoring twelve to fifteen hit points. The clear objective was to prolong the torture.

Kyreen recognized who the lean man worshipped based upon the pendant he carried. Silver on black, depicting a skull in front of a barred gate. Hades clerics were known for their curing capacity almost as much as for their compassion.

She didn't have long to live.

Her torturer, the one asking questions, ones she refused to answer, leaned close. He was decked out in leather armor and his smooth movements tagged him as a thief. He smiled into her remaining good eye. Her other was swollen shut. Pummeling damage. With remarkable clarity she saw his brown teeth, and recalled his foul breath. Her nose, broken and seeping blood—also due to pummeling damage—was long past sensing it. The other detail she'd remember was the jagged scar that bisected his left eyebrow.

"Shortcuff," he said, "my associates have come all the way from Riven Rock. Used a Transport Spell, on the offhand chance they would need to inspire you to divulge what that vile walking corpse, Black Venom, is planning."

Transport Spell? The gray-bearded man standing five steps back was a magic user. A powerful one. At least tenth rank, or less if he read the spell off of a scroll.

Or the man leaning over her was lying.

This was it, she thought. She'd made a good, long run. Longer than the rest of her trapped party.

Through broken teeth, Kyreen said, "Won't tell you…anything." Raw nerves fired sparks of pain with each word uttered. In comparison to what she'd already suffered, the pain was minor. Especially in comparison to what would happen to her, what Black Venom would do if she betrayed him, and the guild.

Other guild members died to keep secrets, had certainly suffered more and longer. No, she wouldn't speak another word.

"Defiance," her torturer said with a wicked grin. "Admirable, but to be expected of a guild's Third Lieutenant." He shrugged, then grinned wider. "Oh, you're thinking that death will be your escape."

This guy was such a flat and predictable NPC. Death *was* her escape. She'd given up on returning to the real world for well over a decade. Since then she'd been loyal to Hermes. She'd given plenty of gold over the years to the church's coffers. She'd frequently plied her trade on behalf of his churches and shrines.

The torturer shook his head, causing his greasy mop of dangling curls to swing. He wiped the blood off his thin dagger onto Kyreen's tattered and already blood-soaked blouse. After sheathing it he pulled a thin necklace from a pocket. It was a silver choker decorated with shards of glittering onyx. He affixed it around her neck.

"Now observe, as my associate prepares your grave and…if you remain uncooperative, where your soul will be tethered." He tapped the necklace and then brushed his knuckles along her swollen cheek. "Say, for a week shy of eternity?"

The torturer backed away as the black-robed Hades

cleric uttered the words to a spell and pointed at her.

Her eye widened as she felt a damp coolness rise up to engulf her body. An instant later, she realized that the cleric had cast a Create Water Spell. The result was a massive quantity of water magically appearing, and she was sinking into the resulting mud.

On instinct, Kyreen held her breath. With her one shattered knee and lacerated tendons along her right arm, and weakened as she was from blood loss, there was no way she could rise up out of what must have been a shallow pool. But urgent panic found away. Her abdomen tightened and she began to sit up, despite the soupy mud clinging to her chest.

The torturer rewarded with a booted kick to the head. She fell back, under the mud again, and without the air the stunning blow forced her to release. Drowning doesn't care if you have one or thirty-one hit points remaining. Being a twelfth rank thief doesn't keep mud from entering your lungs.

The end proved both quicker, and quieter, than Kyreen thought it would be.

Moments later, when Kyreen was truly dead, she felt her soul detach and rise. She floated inches above the silty mud that, as her torturer said, was her grave.

A few well-worded clerical spells by someone associated with her guild would verify she was dead. Unless the same casters expended powerful spells, nobody would know where her grave was. The nearby cleric and magic user could probably make any success in locating her grave next to impossible.

Most thieves didn't end up in graves. Burned to ashes, fed to pigs, weighted down and thrown into a river. That was what unskilled or unlucky thieves expected.

Kyreen had been, unlucky. Missed a saving throw. And now, nobody that she cared about would know that she'd died with honor. That she'd kept the guild's secrets.

Kyreen knew her soul would remain tethered to her corpse for three days, and then she'd be free to join others in the Elysian Fields. She wasn't exactly a hero, but her loyalty to her guild, and to her deity would certainly mean at least an existence along its beautiful border. She gulped, or as much as an intangible soul could gulp, and moved to stand erect upon her grave.

Her eyes widened to see the Hades cleric standing at the foot of her grave, staring right at her. A menacing grin spread across his face.

"That is correct, newly dead thief. You have departed the realm of the living. Departed the working realm of my associate." He gestured to the right where the torturer stood.

The brutal man who'd spent from sunset to midnight causing her agonizing pain gave a slight bow, but his eyes were not focused on her. He couldn't see her.

"You are now in my realm, that of the dead. And from this realm there will be no escape for you." He paused, folding his arms across his chest in an assured manner. "Unless *I* permit it."

Kyreen met the Hades cleric's gaze, undaunted. "I did not tell *him* anything." She gestured to her former torturer.

The predictable NPC torturer didn't acknowledge her words. He couldn't hear her. More than her vanished bodily pain...really she felt nothing. More than the absent caress of the night's cooling air, or the missing scent of the dry thatches of grass tucked next to the sun-baked rocks. More than the mud that should be cooling the soles of her booted feet, the torturer's silence and lack of recognition drove home that she was indeed, dead.

At least her soul appeared to be adorned in the clothing she wore upon her death. It wasn't even torn and tattered. How odd.

After a second's hesitation, the former Third Lieutenant in the Three Hills City Thieves' Guild completed her declaration. "I will not tell you anything."

The cleric stood silent. Amusement crossed his face as he held back what had to be laughter. The utter silence unnerved Kyreen. Except for the cleric, she heard nothing.

"Let us complete our business," the cleric said. "A Converse with the Dead Spell, even when cast by someone as accomplished and learned in the ways of my deity as I am, has a time duration."

Kyreen knew about turning undead. She'd seen clerics do it before. This fellow, she guessed, was at least tenth rank. The volume of water created, and the clarity with which he spoke to the dead suggested that.

But she wasn't undead. Just dead. Without spells, souls couldn't interact with the living, just as her torturer had no real image of her presence. But this cleric could interact with her.

That settled it. Kyreen lunged at him, hands ready to clamp down on his throat.

Mid-leap a force arrested her, like a chained dog. Something around her neck held her back. Her fingers explored around her neck and felt the silvered chain with shards of onyx. She reached back and tried to unclasp it, to no avail.

"What is this?" she asked.

"Why, it is your anchor, newly dead one. True, you are tethered to your body, or would be for three days, but you are now permanently affixed to your grave for eternity...unless *I* choose otherwise."

Kyreen—long ago, back when she was Luci—had never been a Game Moderator. She'd never even looked at the Enchanted Items List in the *Monsters, Maces and Magic* Game Master's Guide. The players who had? They were long dead.

Kyreen staggered back, turned and tried to run. The unseen magical force yanked her to a halt less than a stride from her muddy grave. It wasn't like a collar; more like a full body harness that confined her. Apparently such a magical item existed in the Game Master's Guide, or a homebrewed one created by the SOB Moderator that sucked Luci and her gaming friends into the game world.

The cleric's hands moved to his hips. "You will share with me, what my associate would describe as 'actionable information.'" He turned and nodded toward her former torturer, who could hear the cleric's side of the conversation. "After you do, I will direct him to remove the enchanted item from your neck, that which binds you to your grave."

He shrugged. "If you do not, my other associate will cast a Mud to Stone Spell upon your grave, sealing your corpse beneath the earth. After three days, your soul will *not* be released." He paused and shook his head in mock sadness. "Your soul will then transform into a lesser shade. The weakest of the incorporeal undead.

"And here you will remain, bound to your grave in this isolated wilderness, alone, for centuries upon centuries. If, by some highly unlikely chance a white or gray cleric were to encounter you, and destroyed you, what remains of your twisted and, by then, black soul will descend to inhabit the darkest pools in the realm of

Hades."

He held up his hand with its index finger raised. "You have this final opportunity to share information. For, while I could return and command you as an undead, any information you might reveal will likely not be *actionable.*" The cleric glanced briefly at the torturer. "I have been told, the transformation is a, how shall I describe it? A hollowing experience, as what connection you have to humanity will be consumed along the path to becoming an undead creature."

He placed his hands on his hips again as Kyreen took in what he was saying. Trying to consider if it were true, a half-truth, or a threat without any true teeth.

The memory of a small bronze cross emerged. She'd forgotten about it until that moment. The party's paladin, Roberto the Right, had given it away, to an infant.

What a fool. Ironic, that the party's paladin had been the cause of their entrapment in the *Monsters, Maces and Magic* world. He'd tried to pilfer the remarkably detailed figurine of his character. That really pissed the Game Moderator off.

Her train of thought returned to the tiny cross. It held some enchanted property that protected its wearer from unnatural evil, like undead. If she had it now, she'd be safe.

The cleric's head dropped for a second, bringing her back to the present.

"Occasionally," the cleric said, "my associate fails in his objective. He may not openly admit it, but he is cognizant of the possibility." He glanced with an apologetic look at the torturer. Something which Kyreen surmised was all theatrics for, without a doubt, this cleric was truly evil, and such emotions were not part of his being.

"For *payback* for harming his professional reputation by your refusal to cooperate with him, my associate hopes to leave a lasting unpleasantness as a surprise.

"You see, lesser shades must flee the sunlight. You might guess this parched land enjoys more than its share." The cleric swept an arm wide to emphasize the bleak terrain now under the moon's glow. "Lesser shades, they must return to their grave. What remains of their corpse. True, most have far more range to explore—others would say haunt—than you will. But that is beside the point. The necklace which binds you is silver. As you may know, contact with silver causes pain to many forms of undead. Thus, for the daylight hours, for all eternity, when you are not standing upon your grave, unseen in this barren waste." He again gestured widely around him. "You will be beneath the ground, in your grave. Worse, the enchanted anchor will compel you into what remains of your corpse. There you shall endure the burning agony of silver."

His gaze bored into her incorporeal eyes. "Do believe. I have enjoyed more than a passing acquaintance with undead who are sensitive to silver's touch."

Kyreen stood, frozen and unsure. Was the cleric telling the truth? He had to be. Why would he and the magic user come all this way?

Her reputation for loyalty was unquestioned.

The torturer's people bought off at least four of Duke Hulmer's city guardsmen. Two of the longtime ones she knew in a professional fashion. That familiarity enabled the ambush. Despite that, she nearly slipped the trap's noose, until a cleric's Arrest Movement Spell went off. And she failed her Saving Roll. A one, for sure.

That the city guardsmen were on the take was information her guild needed to know.

She sighed a soul's sigh. She was about to give information that would hurt her guild, the one she'd been loyal to since the age of sixteen. Life—or unlife—out in the barren wastes as a lesser shade? Her instincts told her the Hades cleric wasn't lying. She'd become a lesser shade, and she'd suffer whatever pain an undead could suffer, every day. And every night, confined to the area of her grave? Insects, an occasional desert lizard or rat would be the only diversion. And most animals avoid cursed graves.

Years, if not centuries of such isolation would be torture beyond measure.

She prepared to take the chance that the Hades cleric would follow through on his word. Her now ghostly gut said the chance was less than one in ten that he'd keep his promise to let her soul depart. Attempting to view it from the best angle possible, she smiled to herself. There was one thing she was willing to share. She never liked Higslaff, the pawnshop thief. As a non player character, run by the Game Moderator, he'd been friendly and generous. Once she and her party were in the game, he was far less friendly. She'd overheard him mumble about her being favored. It certainly wasn't true, especially not within the guild. And his maneuvering cost her jobs, and delayed her advancement within the guild.

Higslaff's potential suffering, and possible downgrading within the guild would at least offer her some satisfaction.

"Okay," she said. "I overheard arrangements for an exchange, of an enchanted item to be used to identify covert members of his guild." She pointed a translucent thumb at the torturer thief.

Kyreen spoke quickly, with the cleric repeating the details for the torturer thief to hear. Betrayal felt bitter on her tongue. Even though the bitter taste was her imagination, she just wanted to get the words over with as quickly as possible.

After uttering the last treacherous detail, Kyreen asked, "Is that sufficient for my freedom?" The Hades cleric wasn't the decision maker of the group, but he was the only one of the three who could hear her words.

The cleric turned to the torturer thief. But, before he completed relaying her question, the torturer thief said to the magic user, "Finish it."

The magic user spoke arcane words. Their culmination turned the drying mud of her tomb into stone.

Kyreen Shortcuff had her answer.

The cleric and the torturer stepped to either side of the magic user as he began another incantation. Before the Transport Spell was completed, Kyreen said to the cleric, "You did your job and it wasn't your call." She clasped her hands in front of her and bowed her head slightly. "Remember, you know the location of a minor undead who's learned a tough lesson about loyalty."

The Hades cleric made no sign that he'd heard her. Yet he maintained eye contact until the trio snapped out of sight, either to Riven Rock, or back to Three Hills City, or maybe Shorn Spearhead.

The soul of Kyreen Shortcuff sat down upon her limestone tomb. She began to mentally prepare for the transformation certain to occur, and to manage the feeble thread of hope to escape her fate.

Curiosity tugged at her thoughts, because her mind always tried to locate the best angle in any situation. Would a twelfth rank player character thief transform into an undead more impressive than a lesser shade?

Chapter 1

Higslaff removed his wool felt top hat, careful not to jar the jeweler's double eye loupe as he placed it on his desk. It reminded him of his barber friend, Josiah. His hat and its gear, along with his "Victorian leathers" gave a "steampunk vibe," according to Josiah. Whatever steampunk was. The recently acquired set of goggles strapped to the hat, Josiah described them as reinforcing his "steampunk look." He'd always dressed in that fashion. Procured his first hat at the age of thirteen. Beyond that, the enchanted goggles and jeweler's loupe allowed him to detect magical enchantments and accurately assess gems and their value.

The pawnshop owner scratched his balding head and rubbed his eyes. He was sure dark circles framed them.

Sighing, Higslaff snatched his hat and returned it to its usual perch upon his scalp.

After staring another moment at the leather-bound ledger, he shoved it to the corner of his pinewood desk. There was no good news. The Fireblast attack on his pawn shop had destroyed inventory worth thousands of gold. Add to that the cost of *donating* to the coffers of the Church of Apollo to have his two loyal employees Revived from the Dead.

"Arrogant bastards," he muttered to himself. He rarely had anything good to say about the priests of Apollo. His voice was barely a whisper. The words had no chance of being heard beyond his second-floor office, except maybe by the feline familiar in the showroom below. That meant its master, Coleen Sammae, an enchantress who worked for him, could've heard, too. But the familiar was young, and newly acquired. The Fireblast attack left its predecessor little more than scattered ash and bones. The enchantress would approve of his opinion—the "arrogant bastards." But, without context, she couldn't give the words meaning.

Higslaff thought cats were decent familiars, but not as versatile as a bird. A venomous snake would offer definite advantages as well. Fortunately, he had something that combined both avian and venomous reptile features. And, unlike Coleen Sammae's former familiar, his creature had been on the third floor, in his apartment, during the attack on his shop.

Immediately after the attack, he'd torn out charred timbers and directed the showroom's rebuilding. But business was down. The damn guild war against the thieves of Riven Rock, working to expand into Three Hills City, his guild's base territory, was straight on to blame.

It wasn't *his* guild, except in the sense that the pawnshop owner was a longstanding member who'd slowly climbed the ladder. Middle management. Higslaff held some influence, and protection. Influence or no, when the Guild Master tasked, he completed the assignment.

He stared at the pile of ash next to the burning candle on his desk. He'd read his orders, written in red ink. The words appeared to have been scribed with blood. But the ink didn't affix itself to the parchment like true blood would. He knew that, and knew that Black Venom wouldn't waste blood in such a mundane manner.

That was his second load of bad news. There was a

job he had to see to getting done, and his skilled list of people to handle it was short. Damn guild war. In the last month one shy of a dozen had turned up dead, or missing. Those people he couldn't account for, he'd paid good coin to the witch down the street, to be sure their souls had moved on. One of his people wasn't dead. He paid the witch for a Greater Sending Spell. Even if the lad possessed little knowledge, and nothing beyond Higslaff's cell of the guild, the rival guild having a prisoner wouldn't do. That meant the boy's death. Tendrils of a dark creature of mist, Higslaff imagined, were worse than through the slow ministrations of an experienced torturer. But not by much.

The aging pawnshop owner winced and licked his teeth at the notion. Business was business. And his men did their own killin' and capturing right back. And he'd given payback directly in Riven Rock for the attack on his shop.

He sat up straight as a thought performed a tantalizing dance in his head. Hiring adventurers held risks, but this party had done well for him on a mission. Managed to improvise and succeed where most others of their skill level and talent would've failed.

They were an odd group, but that was the way of those types. He lifted his hat to scratch his head. This adventuring group was well to the far side of the ledger in oddity. And they didn't like him all that much.

He'd need to call in a favor.

CHAPTER 2

Higslaff and Josiah were friends. Well, more like longtime business acquaintances who frequently referred business to each other and lunched together on a weekly basis. Like Higslaff, Josiah was a member of the local thieves' guild. Their lunches allowed them to exchange news and gossip, and ponder their occasional orders from the Guild Master.

The closest thing to a friend either man had.

The *clomp* of Higslaff's boots on the weather-worn planks of the barber shop's porch elicited the usual response from Helga, the barber's gray parrot. "Customer, customer."

Josiah was a lean man, a half head taller than the pawnshop owner. Josiah also had several summers on his friend.

After Higslaff entered, Josiah closed and locked the door to his shop.

The barber preferred browns, from his boots and breeches to his tunic, apron and leather cuffs. Like any good thief, Higslaff noted, as he always did, the outfit made sure the barber didn't stand out. Didn't look particularly dangerous. Higslaff knew otherwise. The sheathed dagger was enchanted, and the man had some skill and training as a thief. Not nearly as accomplished as Higslaff, who'd also done some training as a warrior in his youth. And he preferred the enchanted short sword on his hip to the dagger.

The pawnshop owner thought about his friend. He'd never asked, and Josiah had never shared. But, if he wasn't mistaken, the barber carried some elven blood in his veins. Probably a grandparent's, at most. Only a close and familiar eye might detect the slight point to the ears and higher than normal cheekbones. The man heavily displayed his human heritage, so very few might even guess at it.

Josiah was a thief, yes, but his main trade—besides barbering—was as a lay healer. Not one of any great accomplishment, but he was more competent in that trade than he was as a thief.

"I'll get the tea in the back," the barber said. "What'd you bring for lunch?"

From her high perch near the ceiling, Helga said, "Hot tea. Hot Tea."

Despite what the parrot said, on this summer day, Josiah wouldn't serve it hot. It had been steaming once, but was allowed to cool to room temperature.

While the barber went to the back room, Higslaff closed the shutters to the shop's two windows. Their mesh screens kept bugs out while allowing air circulation. They also allowed conversations to be overheard. The magical light, housed in a small fixture in the ceiling, would be more than enough. The barber shop wasn't a large place. A padded barber chair and headrest sat in front of the big mirror mounted above a counter. Several cabinets with shelves and drawers along the shop's west wall held tools, spare towels and rags, and mundane ointments, oils and salves necessary for the barbering trade. A locked door that led to a closet—what used to be a drop room, until the recent guild war—was built into that wall.

Along the east wall sat four wooden chairs, each with a worn quilted seat pad. Higslaff dragged the customer chairs away from the wall. He arranged two into a makeshift table. The other two would serve their usual functions as seats during the meal.

Higslaff pointed to the tin pail resting on the floor. "Half a loaf of honey wheat bread, strawberry jam, and pickled goose eggs."

Josiah grimaced, returning with two tin cups filled with peppermint tea. Each already had the customary teaspoon of brown sugar stirred in. They'd been meeting for lunch for many years, and Higslaff knew his friend didn't care for pickled eggs. Thus, the familiar grimace. But the pawnshop owner favored their flavor and aftertaste. And it was his turn to bring lunch.

Josiah shared first, about Little Mitchie running afoul of a wererat in the tunnels at the south end of the city. He killed the rat, but suffered a bite. He took to the cage voluntarily, to await and see if he'd been infected.

If the rat did take hold in the apprentice thief's blood, Black Venom might put him down. It depended on how much control over the rodent the human part maintained. Higslaff knew, that with time, a human normally gained ascendancy. But it could take time. And for a long-lived—or existing—undead creature, Black Venom held little patience for such things. With the guild's war losses, the pawnshop owner gave better odds to the Guild Master having patience, if required.

They were halfway through the strawberry jam sandwiches when Higslaff changed the subject. "What's your opinion of the young half-goblin thief, Gurk?" he asked. "And his associates?"

A half smile quirked across the barber's left cheek, stuffed with a bit of his sandwich.

Higslaff leaned back. "Thinking on the busty elf whose legs are longer than mine by nearly half?" The last part was an exaggeration, but not by much.

Josiah nodded, conjuring her image in his mind's eye. "Marigold," he said. "She's got the most symmetrical face I've ever seen."

"Ha!" the pawnshop owner laughed and took a sip of his cooling tea. "Only a barber would notice that." He picked up his pickled egg off the plate. "Why not her long waves of dark hair?"

Josiah lifted his cup of tea. "Because, my friend, symmetry is a key factor in beauty."

Higslaff thought of a few choice comments, but wanted to direct the conversation back to his original question. "She's not the adventuring party's leader."

The barber nodded in agreement and finished chewing his bite of sandwich.

Adventurers, Higslaff thought, and refrained from shaking his head.

The pawnshop owner divided people into three groups. Favored Souls, Mundane Souls, and Souls of Consequence. Most of the city was made up of Mundane Souls. On them the gods paid little heed or favor. Souls of Consequence, which he counted himself among their number. They were movers and shakers, and on rare occasion the gods took notice and meddled in their lives. But the Favored Souls. On those, the gods took notice. He'd witnessed what had to be divine intervention, to shift the odds or alter the actions of others. Sometimes against, but normally to the benefit of a Favored Soul.

Most adventurers were Favored Souls, and he didn't much care to interact with them, unless necessary. How did he know about the gods' intervention? Dealing with such parties in the past, he'd taken action, made deals that he never would've offered. He had no choice, like a marionette whose strings were being manipulated. More than once, one of the gods had worked their will through him, a mere Soul of Consequence.

Gurk's party was made up of Favored Souls. Of that, Higslaff was confident.

The pawnshop owner set his cup of tea on the chair. He took a bite from his pickled egg and placed it on the plate next to his teacup. He was pretty certain that, years ago, Josiah had been a Favored Soul. Not only had his gut and instinct determined it, but he'd once overheard his friend refer to him as an NPC—whatever that was. But it was a term used exclusively by Favored Souls when referring to Mundane or Souls of Consequence.

For some reason, known only to the gods, Josiah had been demoted to a Soul of Consequence. But, having once been one of the more lofty, Higslaff recognized the unusual insights it often lent to his friend.

Higslaff leaned forward, toward his friend, making eye contact. "Can they be trusted?"

Josiah leaned back in his chair and rubbed his chin. "The adventuring party's leader, Lysine, is a druid and also trained as a warrior. I read him as cautious, but an honest individual. The party's other warrior, Kalgore, is impulsive, with a mean streak. Sort of the opposite of the party's gnome healer. He's a tentative fellow."

Higslaff nodded agreement with the assessments. "Most gnomes are. What about Gurk?"

"The half-goblin thief," Josiah said. "Appears to have no intention of joining our guild. Or our opposition," he quickly added. "He appears to be the most inquisitive and knowledgeable about the city. Sort of the opposite of the party's magic user. Maybe it's the elf blood in her, or that being such a beauty, life has been easier on her. But she tends to be on the naive side of the fence."

Josiah reached down and picked up the pickled egg and took a small bite of it. "Why ask me about that party of adventurers. Didn't they complete a job for you a couple weeks ago?"

Out of habit, Higslaff looked toward the door and listened. Then he leaned close. In a hushed voice he said, "Black Venom tasked me to retrieve a magical item that'll assist in the guild war."

"And you're considering hiring Gurk and his party to retrieve it," Josiah said. He knew better than to ask for details.

Higslaff lifted his traveling top hat, scratched his head and sighed. "It'll require a journey. All my people I'd normally assign are engaged in important tasks. Or dead."

"There aren't many adventuring parties in the city at the moment," Josiah said. "From what I can tell, Gurk's party is limited in experience. But they're resourceful." He paused. "Whether they could be trusted with something sensitive?"

"Oh," Higslaff said. "If I hire them, I'll send Snix along—without their knowin'."

Josiah was one of the few that knew about Snix, Higslaff's homunculus. The barber-lay healer had accompanied the pawnshop owner to the wizard's tower where the creature was formed using arcane craft and Higslaff's blood. Higslaff wanted the healing spells on hand, in part for safety and in part to help ensure the reptilian creature bound to him had greater ability to endure damaging wounds and injuries.

Josiah set what remained of his pickled egg on the plate. His friend was very secretive about his minion, and rarely risked the creature. And was considering sending it on a journey. That told the barber much about the importance of what the Guild Master wanted done. The magical components and talent to create such a servant were both rare and costly.

"I learned something that'll be a concern for you," Josiah said. "While getting a haircut, Jax recounted part of an adventure, where he and his party explored a goblin lair in the Dark Heart Swamp. Learned in the storytelling that Lysine, the druid, wears an enchanted crystal around his neck that vibrates when a magical creature comes near. Familiars, undead…maybe a homunculus?"

"Good thing to know, my friend," Higslaff said, his eyebrows arched in surprise, then momentary concern. That was an unanticipated complication. "The warning is much appreciated."

Josiah smiled. "Sharing information for mutual benefit is what has allowed us to prosper." He brushed a crumb from his chin. "I believe the adventuring party you're considering would be reliable," Josiah said, "if they believe they are being paid fairly for the mission."

Higslaff glanced over at the locked door that once led to the clandestine drop room, where guild messages were exchanged. Closed after an attack on the barber shop, just before his pawnshop had been hit. "We've both been pinched in the coin pouch," he said. "That's where you come in."

Josiah raised a skeptical eyebrow as his lean frame tensed.

"They like you far more than me," Higslaff said. "Your part'll be easy." The pawnshop owner held up a placating hand, forestalling any concern. "The half-goblin thief and his party will be more pliable, and affordable, if they come to me for the job, rather than me seeking them out."

Higslaff picked up and examined his half-eaten pickled egg. "You just need to let them know I have a job coming available." He took another bite and savored the flavor. "And see to it that the druid and gnome healer are the ones that come inquiring about the job."

Josiah sat a moment in thought, then nodded once in affirmation. "I can do it. I can get a message to Gurk through the Red Brick. He's taken a fancy to the young serving girl that works there."

Chapter 3

Higslaff sat at his desk, eyes closed as he pondered what items to move from storage to the showroom. Someone knocked on the office door.

He recognized the pattern of three rapid knocks. His nephew, Vernie. "What is it?"

The youth opened the door and peeked in his head, covered with hair the color of damp straw. "There are two men who want to speak with you, Uncle." He spoke quickly, as if he'd just caught his breath. "A dark-skinned warrior and a gnome that carries a cudgel and shield. They're called Lysine and Jax." The youth's eyes widened. "I've seen them in your shop before, and they have friends outside."

"Tell them I'll meet with them shortly. Let them look around the shop for five minutes. Maybe they'll buy something." He began clearing the stack of papers off his desk. "Then escort them up."

"Uh, huh," the boy said. "Five minutes." Then he closed the door and trotted down the stairs.

Higslaff was fond of his nephew, although he rarely showed it. The lad listened well and was eager to learn. Higslaff's younger sister hoped her son would inherit the business, someday. The boy didn't know that. He was just happy he hadn't been apprenticed out to be a farrier or a stone mason, like his older brothers.

When his nephew's boots reached the bottom of the stairs, Higslaff closed his eyes and reached out with his mind, connecting with Snix, his homunculus. Or, as Coleen Sammae called it, his reptilian minion. Despite the magical creature's small size and near to perfect camouflage ability, he knew her feline familiar would eventually catch wind of it. Snix smelled like a damp snake. In addition to a keen nose, a cat's superior eyes and ears would eventually detect it. So he shared his secret. Better than her destroying Snix with a barrage of Mystic Missiles, and injuring its master, in the process.

While the winged creature made its way from the upper apartment down into his office, Higslaff moved two chairs from the worktable and placed them in front of his desk. The homunculus opened and closed the door and flew over to the desk. It wasn't graceful in flight, but the creature's magical nature made it nearly tireless.

Snix was covered in fine scales, like a snake, and physically resembled a cross between a chameleon, a bat and a goblin, shrunk down to eighteen inches in height. Some might mistake it for a devilish imp, except that its prehensile tale lacked the poison barb. Instead, for defense, it bore needle-sharp teeth coated with venom that usually rendered creatures unconscious.

Snix considered himself a *he* because the substance of his essence had been derived from his master, who was a human male. Snix's master thought of him as a *he* or *it* depending on his mood, but never as a *she*. That didn't concern Snix, except for an occasional mild curiosity as to why. The homunculus had access only to those thoughts his master revealed. Even if he desired to, Snix couldn't conceal any thoughts or memories from his master.

Higslaff never had the misfortune of crossing paths with an imp, but he'd once checked the pockets and pouches of a cleric who'd died of a sting from the venomous barb. What stuck with the pawnshop owner was the rank smell of burnt sulfur that clung to the dead priest's body. It was something he'd never forget.

When the pawnshop owner concentrated, he connected in a manner where he could see through the homunculus's eyes, hear with its ears and smell through its nostrils. One of the creature's weaknesses was that it couldn't talk. The closest Snix could manage was gurgles and hisses. But, with minimal concentration, he could carry on a conversation, a sort of telepathy. Snix could poke at its master's mind to initiate a connection, even enough to wake Higslaff from the deepest slumber.

The more distance between them, the longer it took to make a connection—and the more free will the innately mischievous creature seemed to gain.

Higslaff pointed at the long table to the left of his desk, and spoke mind to mind with his homunculus. *Perch over there, far end of the table. Remain quiet and observe. When I say, move to the near end of the table. I've been informed the druid wears a crystal that reacts when a magical creature comes within close proximity. I want to see if, and at what range, you might cause a reaction.*

The homunculus clasped his clawed hands and grinned, showing his pointed teeth. Snix's ability to blend in didn't work on its master.

Higslaff received the mental reply from his homunculus. <I will do as you say, when you say to, Boss.>

Higslaff wanted to see how perceptive the druid and gnome were, with or without the reported enchanted crystal. *Open the door enough that you can slip back upstairs if needed.*

Snix hurried to comply.

A moment later Vernie knocked on the door.

"Send'em in," Higslaff replied.

The druid entered first, followed by the gnome.

Lysine was sturdily built with dark hair, tightly curled and cropped close to his scalp. He stood a few inches under six-feet in height and often wielded a spear, but today only carried a short sword in its scabbard on his hip. The warrior druid wore ringmail armor. All of the rings were bronze, except for two enchanted steel ones, obtained from Higslaff as part of a trade.

The gnome, Jax, stood a few inches over four feet tall, and had thick sideburns and the customary bulbous gnome nose. His heavy boots clomped as he crossed the floor, following Lysine toward the desk.

Higslaff stood and reached across his desk to shake hands with the warrior druid and gnome healer, and then gestured to the two chairs waiting for them.

When they were seated, he tipped his hat back slightly while leaning back in his chair and asked, "Have you come to sell, pawn, or trade an item?" He raised an eyebrow. "Possibly enchanted, like the cursed dagger you brought before?"

"We did not request a meeting for that purpose," Lysine said.

Higslaff expected the druid to speak, but he kept an eye on the gnome.

"We are here to inquire about a job for which you are considering a group of suitable individuals to take on."

Higslaff sat up straight, feigning surprise, as well as sincere interest. "You are?" He dragged out the question as he steepled his fingers. "Might I inquire how you came across this information?"

"Indeed," Lysine replied. "An individual contacted

us through an employee at the Red Brick. It is a tea house."

Higslaff refrained from smiling. Of course he knew what the Red Brick was and he suspected Josiah put his reliable contact in the guild, Josie, up to leaving the message. "Would that person be Josiah the barber?" he asked.

"That would be incorrect."

Higslaff glanced over at Jax and then returned his gaze to Lysine and shrugged. "No matter." The pawnshop owner wasn't sure how far he wanted to push it. He wanted to minimize the chance of drawing a god's interest on behalf of the two Favored Souls seated before him.

"I was going to send Vernie out this afternoon to see if any of my regulars might be interested, but you and your party have done work for me before." He leaned back in his chair again. "And this job is far less…let's say, complicated."

In a lowered voice, Lysine asked, "Does this job involve the conflict between the thieves' guild to which you are associated and the rival guild located in Riven Rock?"

The gnome interjected, "Because we don't want to get drawn into it any more than we already are—have been."

"To be honest," Higslaff said, "the job involves travel. To pick something up and issue payment, and deliver the item to me. It *is* something that will be of assistance in the, conflict, as you call it." He held up an index finger to halt what Lysine, or the gnome, was about to say. In the meantime, he relayed to Snix, *Creep closer on the table.*

<Yes, Boss.>

"I am concerned that you didn't get your information from Josiah, because he is one of the few who know of the planned pick up. What, from the Red Brick, did you learn about the job?"

"That it would pay well in gold and that our party would be well suited for the adventure."

"Nothing else?"

"I assure you," Lysine said, maintaining eye contact. He moved a hand to his chest. After a half second, he tugged on one of the bronze rings, as if to adjust the ringmail armor's position. "Nothing more than what I stated."

The gnome nodded in agreement, although something seemed to be distracting him. His nose scrunched up for a second or two.

"Good," Higslaff said, resting his hands on the table. "I believe that if your party were to leave quietly, and doesn't draw attention, the risk of entanglement would be minimal."

"Further entanglement," the druid corrected. He reached into his satchel and withdrew a small leather-bound book and a pencil.

Higslaff said to Snix, *Back away.*

<Right, Boss.>

Higslaff shrugged his shoulders "What's done is done. If you're interested, I'll give you the details and negotiate a fee for your service." He glanced down at the gnome who rubbed his nose once or twice while looking around. "Is that agreeable, Lysine—and Jax?"

The gnome's attention snapped back to the conversation. He glanced up at his adventuring party's leader. "Yeah, I think we'd like to hear what the job is."

Lysine held up a finger and scribbled a note on one of the small book's pages. He turned the book and placed it on the desk for the pawnshop owner to read.

A familiar may be eavesdropping.

Higslaff studied the note, before quirking an eyebrow at the druid.

Lysine nodded his head once in affirmation.

Higslaff then rolled his eyes. *Sneak close again then quietly retreat back up stairs.*

<Yes, Boss. This is fun.>

The pawnshop owner got up from his desk, opened the door leading downstairs, into the back room holding shelves of labelled merchandise not on display. "Vernie," he called.

The youth bounded up the steps. "Yes, Uncle?"

In a voice loud enough that the druid and healer could hear, he said, "Tell Coleen Sammae her familiar doesn't need to perch on the steps while stalking mice in the storage area right now." His back was turned to the two adventurers as he winked at his nephew. "It belongs up front during business hours."

"Right, Uncle," the boy said and bounded back down the steps.

Higslaff returned to the chair behind his desk, he said, "You are most perceptive, Lysine." He feigned an apologetic look as, out of the corner of his eye, he noted Snix slipping out of the room. "You know that my magic user employee lost her feline familiar in the Fireblast attack."

"We are aware of that as one of the unfortunate outcomes," Lysine said.

"She summoned another familiar, a young feline."

Higslaff did is best to look somber. After sighing, he

said, "I have learned many things during my years as a pawn dealer. But the connection druids have with animals and nature, even within a city." He paused and glanced at the walls, floor and ceiling. "Even within a business establishment built of brick, stone, and wood long years dead."

That seemed to satisfy the druid and healer that Higslaff wasn't aware of the enchanted crystal, and that the triggering was a familiar rather than his homunculus.

Higslaff leaned closer, across the table and whispered, "I liked the previous one better."

The pair of adventurers each offered an uncomfortable smile and redirected the conversation back toward the job.

After sharing preliminary details of the mission and haggling a rough price, the two adventurers made their way downstairs. Before they left the pawnshop, Higslaff went over to the narrow window and opened it. *Snix*, he thought. Higslaff preferred spoken words over mental communication, whenever possible. Now wasn't the time. *Follow them, and stay close enough that you can listen to what they say about the job.* He glanced at the cloudy sky. *But be careful if you have to follow them into a building. Not only is there the enchanted crystal.* He bit his lower lip in frustration. *The gnome, I think, can smell you.*

<Got it, Boss.>

Just as Snix was squeezing through the narrow third floor window and preparing to take flight, Higslaff added, *The elf maiden is a magic user with a familiar. A blue jay.*

Snix mentally hissed acknowledgement and launched into flight.

Chapter 4

The party stood around one of the two tables in the Red Brick, quietly discussing the proposal. The serving girl washed the cups in buckets and placed them on the back shelf. There were very few customers for tea or goat milk in the afternoon, especially with the heat of the day.

Snix clung by his claws to one of the opened shutters that allowed a cross breeze in the small shop, and listened.

"So," the half-goblin thief said, "the dude wants us to go to Shorn Spearhead and pick up some magical item and bring it back."

"Sounds like a cake mission to me," the big warrior, Kalgorc, said. "We just need to follow the main road north. Been there before."

Snix maneuvered to peer into the shop, being careful and moving slowly to maintain proper distance and the advantage of his magical camouflage.

The tall elf maiden huffed, causing her overgrown chest to bounce. Snix knew something like that would distract his master. But it did no more than amuse the homunculus. Every male around the table noticed. Even the dark-skinned druid, who pretended to ignore it.

"If it was easy," the elf said, "he'd have some stupid merchant or man-in-arms go and get it for him."

"It's man-*at*-arms," the half-goblin said. "And we don't know exactly what it is."

"That is correct," the dark-skinned druid said. "In RPG adventures, a common plot element is for an NPC to withhold such details until the basic framework for an agreement regarding the adventure is consented to by the party."

"It's easy money for a week's ride there and back." Kalgore glanced down and sneered at the gnome. "More than two weeks walking at your little waddle-butt pace."

The gnome glared back at the blond warrior wearing breastplate with a scabbarded long sword on his hip. The half-goblin started to say something but the druid placed a calming hand on the thief's shoulder.

"Traveling at such a rate would cause undue fatigue on our mounts," the druid said. He glanced around the table. "In addition, not every party member has opted for the Horse Riding and Handling Skill."

"Yeah," Kalgore said. His gaze shifted from the thief to the elf as he continued. "Some of us took Swimming or Running instead."

The elf maiden tousled the half-goblin's unruly hair. "Some day when you're drowning, you'll be apologizing to my little man."

The thief grinned. "For such a tough guy, Marigold can run circles around you."

"Of course she can." He slapped his breastplate. "I got armor on."

Marigold tucked her hands under her enormous breasts and heaved them up. "And I have these."

"*Monsters, Maces and Magic* takes into account encumbrance due to armor," the druid said. "In addition to the rate of travel by foot for races of smaller stature, such as gnomes. It is fortunate for you, Marigold, the rules that structure this world fail to govern proportionally oversized feminine attributes in a similar manner."

"Yeah," the half-goblin said. "Like my favorite videogames with busty babes."

"Men," Marigold said, rolling her eyes.

"If you are suggesting that men had a disproportionate influence on the rules and art that comprise *Monsters, Maces and Magic* as an RPG," the druid said, "as well as videogame artists and programmers, I believe your assertion is well-founded."

The elf maiden rolled her eyes and puffed out her chest in the young half-goblin's direction. She fake-scolded the goblin thief. "Lucky for you, because these are your fault."

Snix understood the conversation up until the last exchange. While a little disconcerting that he did not comprehend all that was said, his master ordered him to spy and report. Not to understand what he overheard or observed.

The homunculus started to listen in again but a large blue jay flew down and landed on the windowsill. Snix remained absolutely motionless, not even daring to breathe. This had to be the female elf's familiar.

The bird tilted its head, let out a squawk of distress, and launched into the tea house. It landed on its master's shoulder and jeer called at the open window.

"Something startled Petie," the elf said, looking at the blue jay. "What is it?

The elf followed her familiar's gaze toward the window. By that time Snix had already backed around outside and started climbing up onto the roof.

That bird familiar was going to be a problem.

Snix flew high above the city, minimizing his chance of being spotted—by anyone. There were two other homunculi in the city. Like him, they normally worked after sunset. That is what he preferred but, when it came to his will versus his master's orders, his desires were subservient. His master's blood, combined with rare spell components and an arcane enchantment, gave the homunculus both form and life. It tethered him to his master, connected their thoughts. In many ways he was little more than a golem, commanded to do his master's bidding. But he was an enchanted construct with intellect and guile. His master treated him like a familiar, and sometimes coconspirator. His master gave Snix a long leash of freedom and counted on his innate intelligence and cunning.

He was only a few minutes from his master's shop. Still, he knew his master would want what was learned as soon as possible.

Snix reached and tapped at his master's thoughts. *Hssss, Hssss, Hssss.* Three meant he had information that was not urgent.

His master's reply came back before Snix began his spiraling descent toward the pawnshop. <Tell me what you learned.>

The party led by the druid is returning. They desire your gold. More gold than you offered.

The bird familiar sensed my presence. It did not see me and its animal instincts did not recognize me. I evaded further notice.

The druid surmises it was the passing presence of a magic user's familiar. The big warrior dismissed the familiar's alert. The gnome and elf and half-goblin think it was a mistake to discuss their business at the Red Brick.

They talked more about how they should have discussed the adventure at a willow tree near the river instead of the Red Brick, than about your proposal.

They bicker and do not come to agreements easily.

Snix landed on a windowsill of the building that contained his master's business and residence. He slipped into his master's office through the narrow slit of a window. There was a secret entrance on the roof, for which he had a key kept in is small belly pouch. But he only used that at night.

"Ah, Snix," Higslaff said. "A task well done."

The pawnshop owner, sitting at his desk while reviewing a contract, gestured to a clay jar sitting on the corner of the office's table. "A special treat for your effort."

Snix flew over and looked into the jar. The homunculus hissed in delight. Wriggling tadpoles.

"Take it upstairs," Higslaff said in a distracted tone. "Close the door behind you."

Twenty minutes later Vernie tapped his customary three knocks on the office door. He pushed it open to peek his head inside. "Uncle, the adventurers are here. They insist all five come up and talk with you."

Higslaff signaled his nephew into the room. After the youth closed the door he said, "Is that so." It wasn't uttered as a question. "Move the three chairs at my table next to the other two in front of my desk." As he got up, he sent a thought to his homunculus. He felt confident that he already knew the answer. *Which of the adventurers argued the most and who did he argue with?*

Snix replied almost immediately. <The big warrior argued with the female elf, and some with the half-goblin. The druid settled the argument, and the gnome assisted the druid, but sided with the elf and half-goblin.>

He didn't bother thanking his homunculus as his mind shifted to previous meetings with the adventuring party. Humans, elves, and even half-goblins are all creatures of habit. The big warrior, Kalgore would sit on the right, the party's left. Lysine, the warrior druid would sit next to him. Jax, the gnome healer would sit on the left end, nearest the table. His customary spot. The only decision would be where the elf woman, Marigold would sit. Gurk, the half-goblin thief would allow her to choose.

"Pay attention and learn, nephew," Higslaff said. He pulled his dagger from its sheath and went to work splitting the wood and slicing into several of the dowels holding the otherwise sturdy chair together.

He sent his nephew to close the shutters to the office's only window while he finished up.

Move that tall stool over there in the corner next to the table. After you bring the party up, go there and sit.

Vernie hopped to obey, despite the questions Higslaff knew were on the young boy's tongue.

"Do exactly as I say." The pawnshop owner rested a hand on his nephew's shoulder. This would be a first lesson in bartering for the boy. He knew his nephew was loyal. He'd already seen to verifying that, so what was discussed wouldn't leave the room. He'd see if his sister had the right idea about her son one day taking over the business. "I'll explain later."

Five minutes later, Vernie knocked and then ushered the adventuring party into his uncle's office. Higslaff stood and shook hands with each while his nephew shut the door and then sat on the tall stool off to the side.

They had arranged themselves as expected. He looked up to the elf as she sat. She had to be over six and a half feet tall, which meant the chair would be on the small side for her. "Is there a reason you're wearing your cloak's hood up as we meet, Marigold?"

It was a light, cotton cloak, fashioned to wear in warmer weather, and he knew she wore it to hide as best she could her enormous chest and the hood to conceal her remarkably attractive face. While he knew her looks could distract him—they would any healthy man— making her uncomfortable was his focus.

Apparently surprised by the question, she replied, "Uhhmm, my hair is a mess today."

Higslaff shrugged and listened to the elf's chair creak as she put weight on it. "Just to let you know then, that I don't negotiate with people who hide their eyes from me." He quickly gestured to the rest of her party and added, "There are others here. I'm sure they'll speak for you."

Lysine cleared his throat. "It is I, who shall negotiate the final agreement."

The pawnshop owner smiled. "That's fine with me. But why insist on all attending this meeting? Surely they trust you."

"Two heads are better than one, dude," Gurk said, tapping an index finger against his temple.

"I see," Higslaff said. "That's why I allowed your friend, Jax to accompany your party leader when you came seeking the job." He ignored the point that there were five and not two in the office.

"It's because we don't trust you," Marigold said.

Even as she spoke, Higslaff ignored her and continued with a nod of his head toward Vernie. "That is why I often have a second person on my side of the negotiation."

Kalgore laughed. "Before it was because you didn't trust us and needed muscle and steel for backup. Now, you're just insulting us if you say a kid's needed to help negotiate."

Higslaff leaned back in his chair and pushed up the brim of his hat. "How so?"

Kalgore leaned forward, resting a hand on the corner of Higslaff's desk. "Because, I know how these things work. He's here for a reason, and it ain't for helping negotiate."

Lysine rested a hand on the big warrior's shoulder. He did the same when Marigold started to speak.

"Dudes," Gurk said, "let Lysine do the talking."

"Gurk's right," Jax said. The gnome's voice carried a conciliatory tone.

Both the big warrior and elf leaned back. Higslaff noted her chair's wobbling creak, and her effort to keep still. That, he knew, wouldn't last long.

"I must inquire," Lysine asked, "what it is you desire for us to retrieve for you in Shorn Spearhead."

Higslaff straightened in his chair. He adjusted his hat to its normal position on his head. "A Wand of Foe Detection."

His answer clearly riled the group and he knew why. "To be sure," he said, "the enchanted item will be handy in the guild war you know is in progress." He held up his hand, forestalling Lysine's, or any of the other adventurers' response. "The only ones who are aware of the mission's details are myself, my guild's master, and now my nephew. The only other person who even knew I my plan to hire someone to carry payment and bring an item back to Three Hills City was my longtime friend, Josiah." Higlsaff frowned. "And apparently Josie, his trusted messenger."

Kalgore rolled his eyes. "So, what you're saying, is that it ain't exactly a secret."

"Shut up, Kalgore," Marigold said.

"Please," Higlsaff said, glancing up at Marigold. "Since you chose not to pull back your hood, remember that you also chose not to participate in the discussion."

With a huff, she reached up and yanked back her cloak's hood. At the same time the chair's legs beneath her collapsed. The seat of her chair, and her rump resting upon it, hit the floor with a *thump*.

The reactions of Marigold's party members were quite diverse. Kalgore immediately burst out laughing, asking if she'd put on weight. Lysine, with a straight face turned and asked, "Marigold, did your mishap cause injury that requires healing?" Gurk looked down from his seat in surprise, not knowing what to do other than to say, "Whoa." Jax climbed down off of his chair and hurried to help Marigold to her feet, which she brushed off, clearly embarrassed.

Higlsaff snapped his fingers and pointed. In a harsh voice he said, "Vernie, you placed the chairs. Apologize and give Marigold your stool. Now!"

Vernie, a wide-eyed look of surprise, leapt to his feet and rushed to offer his stool.

"Clear away that mess first," Higlsaff said.

Vernie began to comply but being so close to the tall

elf maiden as she got to her feet distracted him. She pushed the gnome away, saying, "I'm fine."

The young boy bent down and began picking up the remains of the broken chair. Marigold bent down to help, distracted by Kalgore's continued laughter. She sneered at the big warrior, then turned back to pick up the broken chair the same instant the boy stood with an armful of splintered wood. The movement buried his face in the elf maiden's pillowy bosom.

Without thinking, Vernie dropped the chair pieces and pushed away from the elf. He stumbled back realizing where he'd placed his hands. Redness shot to his face.

"Leave the kid alone," Kalgore said, still laughing. "You've already embarrassed and aroused him."

Marigold dropped the broken backrest and glared at the big warrior. "You're such an ass." Then she bent over, offering Vernie a hand. "I'm so sorry."

Kalgore leaned close to Lysine and said in the druid's ear, loud enough for everyone to hear, "Tell her he doesn't need another gander at her cleavage. He's just a kid."

The boy, clearly embarrassed, turned away, one hand trying to cover the arousal showing in his trousers. His other hand reached down toward the remnants of the wrecked chair.

Higslaff was around the table, kicking the broken chair pieces aside and placing the stool for Marigold. At the same time, he heard the druid mumble harsh words into the warrior's ear.

Jax picked up most of the broken chair the pawnshop owner had kicked aside.

Higslaff said, "Just drop it over there in the corner."

Then he directed his nephew to stand over by the table. He offered the tall stool to Marigold. "Please," he said, "be seated so we can finish this business."

When Marigold said she'd rather stand, the pawnshop owner leaned close, and signaled for her to bend so her ear was closer. He purposely kept from sneaking a peak down her blouse—which took real self-discipline. "If you don't sit you'll embarrass my nephew further."

With Marigold sitting, uncomfortably perched on the tall stool, drawing attention to herself as she towered over everyone else, Lysine worked to complete the negotiations quickly and lessen his party member's embarrassment.

After the party left, Higslaff called his nephew back up to his office. "Competent job, pretending to be embarrassed," he said to Vernie. He knew there'd been no pretending about it, but he didn't want his nephew to come away from the experience with the wrong lesson.

Vernie nodded once, his nose scrunched up in a mixture of confusion and recalled embarrassment.

Higslaff put an arm around the boy's shoulder. "At the cost of a broken chair, we saved at least thirty gold."

"We did, Uncle?"

"We did," he said. "We made the situation uncomfortable, and made it look like it was their fault. That gave me the upper hand in the negotiations. Although the druid appeared calm and determined, he failed to press as hard as he might for better terms, hoping to end his party member's embarrassment."

Vernie's face scrunched in thought. "It wouldn't have worked as good if it weren't for that big guy on the end."

"Excellent observation, Vernie. And about the elf maiden? As beautiful as she is, her huge breasts, her height. It all makes her stand out. Makes her self-conscious. You, more than anything else I managed, played upon that to our advantage."

The boy shook his head in disbelief. "But she's so…so beautiful."

Higslaff watched as his nephew looked down at his hands, probably remembering where they'd been, what they'd felt. He slapped his nephew on the shoulder and walked back around to his desk chair. "Discord and distraction, and playing on the emotions of the ones you're negotiating with increases the number of gold coins left in your pocket."

He picked up a quill and pointed the feather end toward the corner. "Now gather up that pile of wood and take it over to Spinellie's so he can make me a new one to match. But noticeably sturdier."

While Vernie gathered up the broken pieces, he said, "If she ever meets here again, you're gonna have her sit in the new chair, right?"

"Right, nephew. But why?"

"Make her remember she broke your chair."

Higslaff smiled at his nephew. "She and any party member with her will recall the embarrassing moment. Make them uncomfortable. Knock their confidence." He paused. "Except for the warrior. But he doesn't usually do the negotiating."

After his nephew departed on his errand, Higslaff mentally summoned Snix. While he waited for his homunculus, he pondered how time and events might influence whether his nephew remained a Mundane Soul, or would become one of Consequence.

Chapter 5

Snix used his sharp claws to cling to the covered wagon's underside, tucked behind the rear axle. He wasn't a strong creature. Strength wasn't necessary for stealth. But he was tireless, both mentally and physically. He could hold onto the bottom of the wagon for days, just as he could fly for days. He was neither swift nor fast in flight, and struggled making headway against a stiff twenty mile-per-hour wind.

Being under the wagon kept him out of sight, and remaining in the rear kept him distant from the druid and his crystal. The blue jay familiar flitted about, and scouted ahead. Snix's camouflage worked well, especially in a stable environment. And his primary natural bane against blending in completely was shadows. His enchanted nature could not overcome that obstacle. He worked around it.

So Snix rode and did what he did best: listen and observe.

"You will lose coin on the bricks." It was the gruff yet feminine voice of the hired animal handler, Lilac. The woman was built like a barrel. She wore a chainmail shirt and carried a war hammer slipped through a loop on her broad belt. That was odd for an animal handler, hired to share duty driving the wagon with the druid. Her unruly, but otherwise straight brown hair, didn't quite reach her shoulders. It framed an unremarkable face, except for her nose, which was bent at an angle, probably broken and not properly healed.

All of those pieces suggested Lilac was also hired because she could fight. The road north to Shorn

Spearhead wasn't particularly dangerous, except where it neared the Dark Heart Swamp.

The Brick House was midway to Shorn Spearhead. Snix had stayed with his master twice in the fortress-like establishment. It could be a dangerous place, depending on the travelers lodging in it.

"I told Lysine that," the half-goblin thief said.

He, along with the gnome healer, was sharing the bench seat with the wagon's driver. The big warrior rode ahead on his horse named Four Banger. It didn't appear to be a particularly large or fast mount, but showed to be rugged and reliable.

The druid and the elf magic user were in the wagon. The former was asleep at the front. The latter was tossing and turning. In his experience elves didn't sleep. They entered a detached daydreaming state. Beyond her unusual bodily proportions, the elf maiden didn't have the mannerisms of an elf. If asked for an assessment by his master, he would say that she was probably raised by humans.

After an exasperating sigh the half-goblin, Gurk, continued. "We could've waited for a caravan and joined that."

"Lysine calculated the time versus money," the gnome said. "He thinks time is more important to our mission's success."

As far as Snix knew, the party hadn't revealed the mission's details to the driver.

"Well," Gurk said, "it meant a job for you, Lilac. And good coin in your pocket."

"That's true," Lilac said. "Your party pays good coin."

Jax lowered his gnome voice. "I think Marigold is

happy to have another woman on the road."

Lilac snapped the reins. "A little more coin would've gotten horses," she said. "If time is important, they're faster than oxen."

"Maybe we pay good coin for a driver," Gurk said, "but we ain't nowhere near rich."

His master had given a reasonable advance in gold, and the party of adventurers spent some of it on the wagon, oxen, bricks and supplies.

Snix was to steal back the eight sizable rubies meant to exchange for the Wand of Foe Detection, if the party decided to run off with them. That would be a challenge, since the party split the gemstones among themselves.

And if they decided to run off with the wand, or it was somehow wrested from their control, Snix was to do his best to retrieve it and hide. His master would have to send help because the wand was too large to fit in his abdominal pouch, and his magical camouflage didn't extend to anything he carried outside of it.

The morning blended into afternoon and began to close in on early evening. They'd left behind the small settlements and farms and entered the region not often frequented by guard patrols.

The party was nearing a spot where travelers commonly spent the night, near a stream that flowed close to the road. There was even a small fire pit filled with ashes. Snix prepared to drop off the bottom of the wagon and trail behind rather than risk being detected by the druid or smelled by the gnome.

Seconds after the homunculus dropped onto the road and huddled motionless as the rear wagon wheels trundled past, the blue jay came flying fast on the wing and landed on his master's shoulder. The elf sat next to the druid driving the wagon. The gnome, half-goblin and stocky female driver were asleep in the wagon.

The elf stood up, but quickly sat down again. "Petie says there's humans laying in the deep grass on both sides of the road."

The druid placed a pair of fingers in his mouth and let out a sharp whistle. Watching to see if the big warrior riding fifty yards ahead of the party had stopped, the druid asked, "Are the prone humans dead? Or are they attempting to conceal themselves?"

The bird chirped and warbled.

The elf turned from her familiar to the druid. "Petie says, they are not dead and not asleep, and they are arranged in lines."

"Can your familiar provide the number potentially lying in ambush?"

About that time, the big human warrior had returned and drew his mount close to the slow-moving wagon. "That bird see something?" he asked.

"He spotted an ambush," Marigold said with pride. Then, with a bit of scorn, she added, "His name is Petie."

"How many?" the big warrior asked. "How are they armed?"

The druid replied, "That is what I am attempting to ascertain."

The half-goblin thief shuffled up to the bench. "What's up?"

The elf answered, "Petie spotted an ambush ahead."

"He did?" the thief asked. "And we're still moving toward it?"

Snix flew slowly, keeping pace above and a short distance behind the wagon.

"My objective in only retarding our forward progress

and not coming to a halt," explained the druid, "is to avoid alerting the prone individuals that may intend to ambush us."

"Don't you think whistling me back already done that?"

"How many?" asked the thief, ignoring the big warrior's question. "How are they armed?"

The big warrior snarled, "I already asked that."

The thief threw up his arms. "So what's the answer?"

"What's going on?" the gnome asked.

"Shut up, gnome!" the big warrior growled. "Marigold, you ain't a newbie PC anymore. Tell us what we need to know so we don't end up getting our asses handed to us by a stupid Wandering Creatures Encounter."

Snix flew down, alongside the wagon, maintaining his distance. The elf closed her eyes in concentration, like his master did when trying to recall a vision that Snix had shown him. "Twelve. Six on each side."

"What're they armed with?" the big warrior asked again, working to keep his horse pacing alongside the ox-drawn wagon.

The elf squeezed her eyes closed, scrunching up her nose. "It's hard to tell. Petie flew over quickly. Spears, he saw those. Some leather tubes with feathers—those have to be arrows."

"Quivers," the half-goblin corrected.

In the *Monsters, Maces and Magic* Monster Guide, a band of brigands is frequently comprised of twelve individuals," the druid said. "Often equipped with a variety of weapons."

"Well, there ain't no way they're gonna surprise us," the big warrior said. "And they gotta know we're onto them."

"Your proposed plan of action?" the druid asked.

The warrior said, "We ride up normal until they're close." He gestured to the female driver. "Lilac, here, keeps the wagon going as fast as four oxen can pull it. I ride in and hack them to bits while you all jump out of the wagon and do the same." He paused. "Except for you, Elf. You memorized a Slumber Spell?"

"Yes, and Mystic Missile."

"Okay, that means you'll sleep 1D4 +2 on your side of the road. Then you and the gnome go clean up what's left standing. I'll ride at the other side and take a couple out. Then Lysine and the thief help me mop up."

"Sounds good, dude," said the half-goblin. "When do we attack?"

"The elf's bird familiar—" the big warrior started.

"Petie," she interrupted.

The big warrior rolled his eyes. "When her bird familiar, *Petie*, shows her we're close enough."

"Or," the druid said, "when the brigands rise from their prone position in preparation to loose a volley of arrows toward us."

"Why so pessimistic, dude?" the thief asked. "They'll probably ask us to surrender first."

Several minutes later, with the big warrior still riding his horse beside the wagon as it trundled down the road, Snix observed them getting close to the intended ambush site. The druid and half-goblin were on the bench, on either side of the female human driver. The half-goblin checked the darts in his bandoleer while resting his hand on the grip of his cutlass. The druid had his spear lying alongside him. The elf and gnome were beneath the canvas of the covered part of the wagon.

Off to their right a big crow feasting on the carcass of a recently killed groundhog cawed and took flight. At the same time the blue jay familiar, two-hundred feet in the air, circled to return.

"That's it!" The big warrior pulled his sword and kicked his horse into a gallop.

He angled to the left while the druid and half-goblin leapt from their seats onto the deep grass that lined the hard-packed road. The elf leapt out of the back, onto the road. She jogged along and helped the gnome as he nearly tumbled out after the driver snapped the reins to get more speed out of the normally lumbering oxen.

The big warrior closed to forty yards when a whistle brought all of the brigands, hidden on both sides of the road, to their feet. They were dressed in mixed types of armor, but mostly along the lines of leather or a mail shirt. All but one were armed with bows, now drawn back and ready to fire their arrows. One gray-bearded brigand raised his staff and shouted, "Fire!"

Several arrows pinged off the big warrior's breastplate, and one off his helmet. One arrow, however, buried itself in his mount's shoulder. The horse slowed but continued forward. That side of the road ignored the charging druid and thief.

On the other side of the road, the gnome held his wooden shield high, trying to protect the elf crouched behind him. She was speaking the words to a spell.

She completed her incantation the same instant the

six men loosed their arrows. Three collapsed to the ground like damp sacks of wheat. The elf shouted, "Ouch! Why do they always shoot me in the boob?"

Right after that the man with the staff completed his spell. The big warrior and his mount dropped to the ground like those across the road, but harder as they were moving fast.

Brigand shouts filled the air. As the druid and half-goblin charged they both yelled, "Magic user!" Each brigand nocked another arrow.

The druid hurled his spear and the half-goblin threw a dart while on the run. The spear struck the magic user a glancing hit on the thigh, and the dart caught an archer in the cheek. Five arrows came back at the adventurers from point blank range. The thief dodged both aimed at him. The druid took one arrow in the shoulder. He drew his short sword and ran past the slumbering warrior and his mount.

On the other side of the road the gnome charged as the elf trotted to keep pace behind him. She stopped and looked up. "Petie!"

In the air above the blue jay was locked in an aerial fray with a big crow. It had to be the enemy magic user's familiar. The crow was bigger and stronger, but not as nimble in the air.

Snix ascended toward the battling birds as they lost altitude. The blue jay made his spying job harder, but was an asset to the party. They might need him later, once they got his master's wand.

Only two shot arrows at the elf and gnome. One had taken to slapping a fellow brigand and shouting for him to get up and fight. The gnome's shield proved effective in deflecting one arrow, and the magic user used an unexpected move. She knocked the arrow aside with a well-timed sweep of her hand. Snix had never seen a magic user do that before.

Letting the gnome continue on forward, the elf turned and cast a second spell. A single pink mystic missile shot from her pointed finger across the road and struck the enemy magic user.

The magic user redirected his spell at the elf. Two glowing gray mystic missiles struck her. She backpedaled a step but didn't go down. Neither magic user was powerful, but the brigand was stronger than the elf. Again, Snix was surprised. The elf was still standing, despite an arrow wound and two mystic missiles.

The homunculus took a moment's attention away from the battle on the ground and focused on the two birds now less than ten yards away. Snix knew that in a fight, his claws weren't very effective against creatures the size of humans. But he was bigger than the crow, and he could easily tip the fight's balance.

He only needed to adjust his position by a few feet. When they came into range he struck out with a claw and came back with black feathers. He immediately shook his hand to loose the feathers from his claws.

Wounded, the crow *cawed* and went on the defensive, with the blue jay getting above and behind, and pecking down. The crow dove and swooped to his left, the blue jay followed, jeer calling.

Back on the ground, the druid and half-goblin thief were in the middle of a melee with the magic user and five brigands. Bows had been discarded in favor of maces and hand axes. The two adventurers stood back to back. While that offered a better defensive position, it limited the thief's use of his speed and quickness to dodge.

On the other side of the road, four brigands surrounded the gnome healer. He suffered several mace strikes, but managed to take down one brigand with his cudgel. The elf entered the fray, missing with her rapier but drawing off one of the gnome's attackers.

Concern flowed into Snix's thoughts. The battle could go either way. He began to consider how he'd steal the rubies back from the brigands.

The battle continued. The gnome had dropped another brigand, but suffered another solid blow. The elf wasn't able to lay steel to her foe's flesh, but neither did he managed to connect with his hand axe.

The druid and half-goblin each dropped a brigand, but the druid was down on one knee.

Then, without a battle cry or warning, the female animal handler entered the fray. Her war hammer connected with the magic user's skull. Staggered, he missed a counter strike with his staff and paid with a solid blow to the ribs. He went down.

The elf went down and the gnome rushed to her aid.

Instead of pursuing, the gnome's foe turned and kicked his two slumbering partners awake.

Cries of battle turned to cries of retreat. Five brigands fled all directions. The half-goblin began to pursue but returned when the druid called to him.

Snix noted that while the adventuring party's pre-combat organization was poor, after the battle, action was completely different. The gnome healer was able to take both the druid's and the elf's wounds upon himself, and heal most of the damage. The druid was able to use his healing to cure the horse's arrow wound and most of the half-goblin thief's injuries. The thief searched the bodies while the blue jay familiar located the brigand campsite three hundred yards away. The thief and elf gathered abandoned gear while the familiar flew high overhead, watching the fleeing brigands.

Several of the fleeing brigands took what was of value from the camp and made for a distant stand of trees.

In the meantime, the big warrior managed to strip the bodies of their armor and weapons. He tossed the corpses behind a rise so that they wouldn't be spotted from the road. He grumbled the most. The druid stood watch while the female driver loaded the fallen brigands' weapons and gear into the wagon.

In under fifteen minutes, the adventuring party was back on the road, working to put some distance between themselves and the scene of the battle.

Snix flew along, keeping his distance. He'd reported in to his master. Higslaff asked few questions and commended the homunculus's covert assistance.

Minutes before sundown, the party pulled off the road and onto a flat area with patches of deep grass and scattered rocks. Snix saw no preparations for a fire, so it was going to be a dark camp. The moon was nearing full and scattered clouds would offer some visibility to the humans. Elves, gnomes and half-goblins saw better at night than humans, but not as well as a homunculus.

After the druid and driver tended to the horse and oxen, the party gathered in a circle and ate a meal of cheese, bread, dried goat meat and drank water while the driver stood watch in the fading light. The blue jay, still suffering from wounds inflicted by the crow, also stood watch, but from atop the wagon.

The homunculus hunkered down near the camp, between two rocks and listened to the conversation.

"So, what do ya think?" the big warrior asked.

The half-goblin grinned. "I think the fight would've gone better if our best warrior hadn't gone down right at the start."

"Listen here, thief," the warrior said. "It could've taken out any one of us."

"Except for Marigold," the thief corrected. "Remember, elves have innate resistance to Slumber Spells." The half-goblin's croaking voice held humor. He clearly enjoyed poking fun at the big warrior.

"Gurk," the druid said in a sharp tone. "Kalgore is correct. Furthermore, the magic user clearly targeted Kalgore and his mount."

"Why do you say that?" asked the gnome.

"Because," the half-goblin said, "a Slumber Spell affects 1D4 +1 per rank of the caster, beyond first rank. He was at least third, maybe fourth rank."

The gnome stuffed a piece of bread in his mouth and asked, "How do you know that?"

"Marigold saw his Mystic Missile Spell, up close." The big warrior gestured toward the elf. "Ask her how many missiles hit her."

"Two," she said. "I'll get my second missile when I get enough experience points to reach third level."

"Rank," the half-goblin and big warrior said in unison.

The elf huffed and rolled her eyes. "Whatever."

"It is quite fortunate that you have Byeol's eight hit

points available," the druid commented. "A second rank magic user. Normally could not withstand 1D4 +1 and 1D4+2 points of damage."

"Plus, they shot you in the boob with an arrow," the gnome added.

"In the chest, Jax. Why did you have to say boob?"

The gnome looked down at the ground. "It's exactly what *you* said," he mumbled.

The elf did her best to cross her arms over her chest. "I had to use Byeol's Warrior Monk moves to block arrows they shot at me, so I lost out on experience points, *again*."

"Better than being dead," the half-goblin said.

The elf's hand tapped at her left boot, just above the ankle. "She hates being trapped in that gem."

"It is alexandrite," the druid said.

"It's an alexandrite Soul Stone," the half-goblin thief said. "And it's better than her soul being gone—wherever it would go in this world."

"It might've gone back to our world's heaven," the elf maiden said, sadness in her voice.

"Yeah," the big warrior said. "But if we get back, and take her soul with us, she might..." he looked over at the druid. "What'd you call it?"

"Reconstitute."

The warrior slapped the druid on the shoulder. "Yeah, that's it. She might reconstitute back into herself, just like we will."

"If there's any getting back," the gnome said glumly.

After popping a small slice of cheese into his mouth the druid adjusted his sitting position. "If I accurately recall, there is a ten percent chance for a band of brigands to have either a cleric or a magic user, 1D6 in rank, as their leader." He looked at each of the party members in their small circle. "Or, it was not a Wandering Creatures Encounter that we experienced. Rather it may have been a failed ambush based upon knowledge of our mission for Higslaff, the Pawnshop Owner."

The big warrior spat onto the dry grass. "If you guys wouldn't've let the Slumbered brigands get woken up to get away, or captured instead of killing every one that didn't run." He smacked a fist into his palm. "We coulda found out."

"Hey, dude," the half-goblin said, "it was a pretty tight fight, up until the end. We were all pretty cut up, missing a lot of hit points."

"I know," the big warrior said. "Sucks that magic user got his spell off."

"That's not the magic user I'm worried about," the elf said. She looked at her party members, then over her shoulder. Her voice dropped to a whisper. "I'm worried about the lich."

"That zombie with the Tracking Gem spotted a fairy with the Soul Stone," the half-goblin said. "Heading toward Riven Rock." He reached up and rested a hand on the elf's shoulder. "You ain't a fairy anymore, and we're never going back to Riven Rock."

The gnome said, "But, Kalgore shouted Marigold's name."

The big warrior threw his hands up in the air. "You always gotta bring that up, don't you, gnome. Marigold was panicked and I had to tell her what to do so I could hack the zombie up."

The druid held out his hands in a calming gesture. "We all agreed that the leprechaun's Transmorph spell, and the direction of travel has thrown off pursuit."

"Yeah," the half-goblin said. "And I bet a lot of fairies are named after flowers."

All in the party nodded in uncomfortable agreement.

In silence, they hastily finished their meal.

CHAPTER 6

Higslaff found his homunculus's report interesting.

Certainly, the ambush came from a band of brigands, intent on looting any worthwhile target traveling on the road. A single wagon would normally be an easy target. How often does such a wagon carry a party of adventurers—a group of Favored Souls?

The brigands got what they deserved, taking advantage of the guild's temporary inability to extend its influence beyond Three Hills City due to the guild war.

But a Soul Stone? Now that was *very* interesting. And the lich seeking it? Liches, thankfully, were extremely rare. Worse than dragons. The only one he'd heard whispers of supposedly had an isolated stronghold deep in the Dark Heart Swamp. Malthia the Cursed was the name not mentioned—at least not by those with any brains.

The half-goblin thief, Gurk, and his party traveled twice on adventures into the Dark Heart Swamp. Once on behalf of the Church of Apollo, and the second time for the silversmith, Timz Simman. He'd have to get more information on those adventures. The silversmith would be easier than the Apollo Church.

Higslaff pondered. He had a good working knowledge of enchanted items. It was necessary for success in his line of work. Getting ahold of such a stone could benefit him greatly. Offer him abilities he'd only dreamed of. Better yet, the sale of such an item would bring wealth and valuable favors.

Certainly, a powerful, spellcasting undead creature like a lich would crave such an enchanted item. But there was no way he'd ever initiate dealings with a lich. He'd be reduced to a pile of ash, scattered by the next breeze, before negotiations even began.

But, there might be other options…

Chapter 7

The adventuring party was up and moving before dawn. Except for the driver and the elf, all were groggy and slow moving. The elf had taken part in two shifts of the double watch, since she needed no sleep, and the driver didn't participate in any of the watches.

Shortly after sunrise the druid cast a curing spell upon the gnome and the blue jay, removing all evidence of wounds from the previous day's fight. From then on, the travel went much as before, with the druid and big warrior trading shifts on the horse, and a lot of sleeping in the wagon when not watching for further ambushes.

They drove their four oxen hard. Their objective was to keep ahead of any escaped brigands reaching the Brick House before they did. The druid and big warrior were convinced any organizer of the ambush in the area would use that as his base of operations.

Snix had to admit, it was a reasonable theory. The Brick House attracted all sorts of travelers, and many of the less lawful types. Many meetings and deals were made there, out of the sight or hearing of city guardsmen or church leaders.

It wasn't an establishment frequented by common merchants and members of caravans, unless in sufficient numbers and well-armed. Those deemed vulnerable were more often beat up and stripped of valuables, than accepted within the fortress-like waystation. It hadn't always been that way. Snix's master didn't know why Duke Huelmer allowed the place to become hostile to common merchants. Three Hills City depended on trade for continued prosperity. The only other route, via the

Snake Claw River, was unreliable during the winter months.

Three hours after sunset, the party reached the Brick House. They stopped at the well house across the road from the red-brick structure. It was really a series of buildings creating a central courtyard. The outer wall, formed by many of the buildings was both thick, and high, and the wide entry gate was currently closed, and guarded. The small gate was also guarded, but would allow those willing to enter, or leave, to do so.

The party established a camp among several other scattered caravans. The gnome and big warrior casually stood watch while the druid and driver tended to the oxen and horse. The elf and half-goblin set up the camp.

Snix listened while elf and half-goblin did so.

The elf handed down the canvas sheet to the half-goblin. The party used it to make a small A-frame tent since there wasn't enough room in the wagon for all to sleep. Especially with the brigands' captured weapons and gear.

"You really think it's a good idea to stop here?" she whispered.

"Yup," he whispered back. "Past here, the road runs along the eastern edge of the Dark Heart Swamp."

Experience taught Snix that both elves and half-goblins had hearing superior to a human's, almost as good as his. From his position a dozen yards from the wagon, he needed to listen carefully to hear their conversation.

She nodded understanding before going back into the wagon to get the tent's poles and iron stakes. "We got in that big fight here last time, remember?"

"I do, but we gotta rest our oxen and Kalgore's

horse." The half-goblin followed the elf to the wagon. "We'll get up and going before sunrise."

The elf hopped down, carrying the poles and a sack that held the tent's cords and iron stakes. With her long legs, it wasn't much of a drop. Still her chest bounced, drawing the half-goblin's attention.

He quickly looked away, apparently embarrassed.

The elf helped unfold the tarp to set up the tent next to the wagon. "Arrive late, leave early. That way we won't be noticed?"

"Nah, dudette." The thief grinned, pulling the contents from the sack. He looped the cords over the ends of the tent poles and handed one to the elf. "But they'll have to make their move tonight, or have to play catch up tomorrow."

"And you'll be ready for them, my little man." She reached over and tousled his hair.

"Hey, don't do that." He pushed away her hand. "I already ain't got a comb."

"Wanna look handsome for the bad guys?" She went to the other end of the tent to set her pole. "I'll lend you my comb." She held the pole in place.

"Better not," the half-goblin said, still whispering. He looked around while stretching the tent and pushing in the stakes in with his boots. He spotted where the big warrior stood watch and jerked a thumb his direction. "Kalgore'll get jealous."

The elf giggled. "Let him."

Josie showed up at Higslaff's shop several hours after nightfall. The pawnshop owner had retreated to his top-floor apartment to relax and read from a text chronicling the last century of the Morrin Confederacy, rival of the Agrippa Empire. Most would say they were enemies, and Higslaff counted himself amongst the majority.

Three Hills City was on the outskirts of Vandike, one of the lesser kingdoms within the Morrin Confederacy. Across the Snake Claw River, after a small uninhabited region, the Agrippa Empire began. Riven Rock was within that hostile empire. Higslaff suspected the centuries' long conflict influenced the incursion by the thieves' guild in Riven Rock.

Higslaff picked up the book and removed the silver bookmark etched with a picture of a unicorn on one side and a sea serpent on the other. He was halfway through the book. He'd purchased it five years ago from a sage's assistant who was travelling through town. Nervousness of the assistant, and the low price he demanded hinted that it was stolen from the sage's collection. Higslaff purchased it, knowing the theft wasn't his problem.

The book's history ended twenty winters prior to current events, so it wasn't too far out of date. He'd temporarily exchanged it with Keri Lovelace for a book detailing the cultures of satyrs and centaurs. She, like him, maintained a personal library.

"Mr. Higslaff," someone shouted up the stairs. The closed and locked door muffled words.

Higslaff got up from his desk and grabbed a scabbarded, enchanted short sword. Nothing fancy or remarkable, just a lesser enchantment making it more effective in striking and wounding. Still, it had cost him plenty of coin, even though the adventurer had been desperate for gold.

He unlocked and opened the door a crack. Seeing the hired guard inside the doorway, looking up the narrow stairwell, the pawnshop owner opened the door further.

"Yes?" he asked, trying not to sound annoyed. He'd hired two men-at-arms to watch his shop at night. Part of the price he paid for Snix's absence. The guards weren't too expensive. They also would do little to deter a determined theft attempt, or attack by the Riven Rock Guild. But they kept away small riffraff, and their deaths might provide warning, and time, for the pawnshop owner to take action. Save his business, or his life. Or both.

The inside guard announced, "Gordie, outside, says there's a woman that wants to talk to you. Says her name is Josie."

"Thanks," Higslaff said. He lifted his hat from a hook next to the door and started down the steps. Josie wasn't one of his contacts. She worked with a number of merchants either in or that supported the local thieves' guild, like Josiah. With the losses to the guild, her territory and responsibilities must've been expanded.

Higslaff followed the inside guard down to the first floor. He pulled the enchanted short sword from its scabbard and motioned for Wenz to ready his mace. Higslaff thought about having Wenz open the front door, but it was unlikely he would recognize Josie. The guard went to do it anyway.

Normally Snix would've been in position to allow the pawnshop owner to scope out the situation and verify it was Josie.

"You open," Higslaff whispered. "I'll see if it truly is

Josie."

After Higslaff unlocked the door, Wenz opened it a crack. The guard kept a shoulder leaning against it, ready to force it closed. Unlike some merchants, Higslaff paid a little more coin to ensure competence.

The pawnshop owner recognized Josie's outline in the shadowy light created by the scattered post-mounted Light Spells. "Thanks, Gordie," Higslaff said to the guard standing behind her on the porch. "Come on in, Josie."

Josie stepped in. Higslaff slid the sword back into its scabbard. He locked the door.

Higslaff nodded once to Wenz and said to the female thief, "Follow me up to my office."

Josie was cute, with freckles and sparkling green eyes. Higslaff thought she was a little on the chubby side. She was dressed in a brown linen blouse and wool knit pants that reached mid-calf. She'd stick out among the desperate poor, but blend in with some of the middle-class merchants and their families. Her sandaled feet were dusty. She'd done a lot of walking.

She took a seat in a chair in front of Higslaff's desk and pushed aside a curly auburn lock dangling in front of her right eye. After adjusting the position of her sheathed dagger for comfort, she began. "I'm to inform you that Kyreen Shortcuff is dead. Galthorn believes her soul never departed, and is still earthbound. Where?" She shrugged her shoulders and scrunched the left side of her face. "Probably we'll never know."

"Thank you for coming," Higslaff said. "Is, not knowing her soul's fate, Galthorn's assessment?"

She said, "This came straight from Black Venom."

"I see."

"Not telling you something you don't already know,"

Josie said. "She was a tough cord, not easy to snap. But..."

Higslaff tipped his hat's brim back. But, being high up, she knew a lot. That was the unspoken message. The pawnshop owner waited. Protocol stipulated that Josie had certain information to share, and she would. Asking questions to prompt for additional details was impolite—or an insult to some. Josie was easygoing, so impolite.

"I was told treachery by some in the City Guard is how they nabbed her."

That statement really piqued Higslaff's interest. That the rival guild somehow ensnared her was obvious. The City Guard were known to be hard-asses, but not corrupt.

Josie said with certainty, "Families suffer for treachery performed."

That, like everything else, was an indirect assertion of Black Venom, to be shared. Not suffering caused by her—Josie's—decree or action. Dealing with the guilty guardsmen directly would cause reprisals. The indirect payback might cause some reprisal, due to orders from higher up the chain of command. But those guards down at the lower ranks? They talked among themselves. They'd know the score.

Josie tugged on the sleeves of her blouse. "That is all I have to report. Is there any message that you'd like carried back?"

"Due to a scarcity of guild reliables," he said, "I have hired a proven adventuring party to retrieve the Wand of Foe Detection for the guild. They are en route to the pickup. I anticipate their return within a week."

He didn't need to add that Kyreen Shortcuff knew of

the task assigned to Higslaff. If she spilled the beans on it, the opportunity for the Riven Rock guild to intercept the delivering party or the adventuring party sent to retrieve the wand increased significantly.

"Would you like a cup of wine, water or cider, before you go back out, onto the streets?"

That offer told the female thief that the pawnshop owner had no other messages for her to relay. She stood and declined the offer with a hand gesture. "I have more people to meet tonight."

Higslaff stood and walked around his desk, toward the door leading downstairs. "Maybe another time, and place. I'll by the first round."

"Sure," she said.

The pawnshop owner could tell she was already thinking about her next destination, possibly considering if she should alter her intended route. It's what he would be pondering.

Higslaff put the history book away and prepared himself for bed.

Although Shortcuff was a skilled member of the guild, and her loss would be felt, he wouldn't miss her. She was a Favored Soul. He didn't appreciate the grief they often brought. He also knew that, although the gods tended to favor and watch out for them, Favored Souls tended to meet with violent ends.

He thought about using Snix to warn the adventuring party. A vague warning, where he couldn't provide details related to the guild, seemed unproductive. He had no idea of how or if the rival guild would take action—if they learned about it from Shortcuff. She knew a lot more of value than the most recent mission he'd been assigned. Even so, he'd have to hire a third guard.

The adventuring party held a significant head start on anyone the rival guild might dispatch to take the Wand of Foe Detection for themselves.

He slipped the thick tome of history on the shelf. Lysine and his party would make the pickup. He dismissed the failed brigand ambush as originating from Riven Rock. Any chance at interception would happen while returning from Shorn Spearhead.

If the situation changed, he *might* order Snix to reveal himself, and relay a warning. That coming need seemed unlikely. Lysine was an observant leader, and Gurk was resourceful.

Besides, they were all Favored Souls.

Nobody bothered the party during the night. They watered and fed oats from the wagon to their oxen and horse before moving out ahead of the other two caravans that decided to form into one. Through casual conversation, the big warrior learned the combined caravan was heading toward Three Hills City.

The morning passed slowly as the party trundled north. The big warrior kept his mount on the west side of the road, nearest the Dark Heart Swamp. When they stopped for lunch and to rest the oxen and horse, Snix landed and hid behind a prickly bush.

The party began bickering about what was purchased for the food rations and what would've been better.

Snix snatched a field mouse that wandered too close and popped it into his mouth. Due to his enchanted nature, eating wasn't necessary for survival. It was, however, something he enjoyed—if the food was right. Tadpoles were the best, just ahead of earthworms, followed by chicken eggs a day or two before hatching. Field mice were a treat, since the pawnshop's familiar tended to catch them, and didn't share. Maybe the new familiar could be persuaded, or intimidated?

The blue jay began jeer calling an alarm. He was looking right at the bush Snix had settled behind, feathers ruffled.

"Petie sees something," the elf said. She looked up at the bird perched atop the wagon. "What is it?"

Snix slowly began to back away. The noon sun was up, with no cloud cover. Despite blending in, he was casting a shadow. Tucked close to the thorn bush, that didn't matter.

"Over there." The elf pointed. "Around that bush." Her keen elven eyes were trained his direction. The half-goblin had his cutlass drawn and was moving toward the bush from the right. The druid, with spear in hand, was coming from the left. The big warrior, for some reason, had pulled out his short bow and nocked an arrow.

Snix wiped the faint tracks his clawed feet left in the dry dirt. They weren't much, but the druid or thief might detect them.

He scuttled backwards, behind a clump of grass and

hunched down.

The bird jeer called another alarm. The elf said, "I saw it too—I think." She drew her rapier and strode forward.

The druid and half-goblin thief were moving up, getting close. Only thing to do was to take flight and hope for the best.

"Describe what you observed," the druid said.

"There—huh?" the thief said. He sprinted forward and pointed his cutlass where Snix had been. "I saw something. Like a gray spot, or shadow."

"Shadow of what?" the big warrior asked, looking around in the sky.

"I dunno, dude." The thief poked his cutlass into the patch of grass. "Weird."

The party remained extra vigilant the rest of the day, watching for shadows. Snix kept his distance, even during the night, being especially wary of the elf and her familiar. As a result, he was only able to listen in on bits of conversation. After his previous reporting, his master wanted to know more about the adventuring party, so having to remain at a distance was a problem.

He'd have to do something to distract the elf and her familiar.

Chapter 8

Late afternoon was sunny and hot, but distant dark clouds in the West hinted at possible storms. After scouting ahead, the big warrior came riding back at a gallop. "Stop the wagon!" He didn't shout the words, but there was urgency in his normally confident, if not boisterous voice.

The female driver pulled on the reins, bringing the wagon to a stop. Several hundred yards to the left was a small stand of trees. Otherwise, thistles and grass covered the flat terrain. The faint odor of decaying vegetation wafted in the breeze coming from the west, from the Dark Heart Swamp.

From his seat on the bench the druid asked, "What did you observe?"

"Dire Boar." The warrior turned his horse to face back up the road. "Must've come from the swamp. The wind ain't carrying our scent that way, is it?"

Normally unflappable, the female driver's eyes went wide.

The gnome, sitting on her right, opposite the druid, looked from the big warrior to the druid and back.

"The breeze has tended from west to east the vast majority of the day," the druid said, now standing. He apparently spotted the beast. "It will take notice of us visually long before our scent might reach his olfactory system."

The elf, resting in the wagon, stuck her head forward. "What is it?"

The gnome looked back, getting a face full of elf bosom.

The elf shifted position. "Sorry, Jax."

"Dire boar," the gnome said.

"Dire what?"

The half-goblin stuck his head forward and asked, "Did someone say dire boar?"

"Yeah," said the big warrior, pointing north.

The elf turned to the half-goblin. "What's a dire boar?"

The half-goblin squinted his eyes, not yet adjusted for the sun. "Ever heard of a hogzilla?"

"No."

Not taking his eyes from the distant creature, the druid explained. "Hogzilla, in some parts of the United States, is a colloquial term for an abnormally large feral swine, or hog."

"A warthog, like Pumbaa," the elf said. "Only bigger?"

"Dire boars are like hogzilla's bigger, meaner brother."

"Oh, I see it now," the elf said. "It—it's bigger than one of our oxes."

"Oxen," the druid corrected. "Dire Boars are nine hit-die creatures. If I recall, from the Monster Guide, they are foul-tempered beasts. Omnivorous, but with a preferential taste for the flesh of dwarves and cattle."

In a matter-of-fact voice, the big warrior said, "They're meaner than a hungover sorority girl with PMS."

"That was rude." The elf leaned on the gnome's shoulders, knocking his head forward with her chest.

The half-goblin snickered. "Come on, Marigold. That was Kalgore talking."

"Stop flirting with the gnome, Marigold," the big

warrior said. "This is bad. Lysine, you think we should work on turning the wagon around? That thing's sort of wandering our way."

"There's five of us," the gnome said. "Six, if we count Lilac."

The driver glanced down at the gnome, a look of disbelief on her face.

The druid climbed off of the bench and hefted his spear. "Once a dire boar strikes successfully, it has a ninety percent propensity to attack the same target the next combat round."

"Dude, each tusk does 3d4 damage." The half-goblin followed the druid down. "That's an awful lot for second and third rank characters."

"This Wandering Creatures Encounter sucks." The big warrior climbed off his mount, which had started to snort and show signs of panic. "Which means if it comes to a fight, we'll eventually kill it." He led his horse to the rear of the wagon and began lashing its reins to an iron loop.

The gnome gave the driver an apologetic glance before climbing down. "But it'll probably kill one of us in the process."

CHAPTER 9

Snix spiraled down and landed on the dire boar's broad back. Coarse bristles covered the huge feral swine's thick skin. The homunculus grabbed onto a few of the bristles and hung on.

The wagon's turn focused the dire boar's attention in the party's direction, but Snix had to agree with the big warrior. The coming fight—the so called Wandering Creatures Encounter—was inevitable. Snix wasn't sure why, but instinctively he knew it was.

The homunculus found it impressive that the party didn't abandon the oxen, scatter and hope for the best. He didn't understand the reference to ranks and experience points. He'd heard them mentioned before, and would share that with his master.

The dire boar didn't seem to notice, or mind, having something on its back. Snix opened his mouth wide, exposing his needle-like teeth. His venom wouldn't affect the big creature, but maybe his bite would distract it enough to ignore the party and its oxen.

The homunculus bit down. It probably hurt like a horse fly hurts a horse. The big boar grunted, then dropped and rolled over onto its back. Snix leapt away and launched into the air before getting crushed.

The party watched the approaching creature suddenly

grunt and then drop and roll onto its back, and roll around. It got up and repeated the action. After getting to its feet again, it spun around twice, snorting and grunting at the air above it.

"Dude," the half-goblin said to the druid. "Can dire boars get, like, rabies?"

For a second, the big boar started to run southwest, back toward the swamp. Then it stopped and stuck its snout up in the air.

"The wind direction has shifted," the druid said. "Enact Plan A."

The big warrior rolled his shoulders beneath his armor. "I knew it."

"Plan A?" The half-goblin spat onto the dry earth. "You mean Plan Sacrifice the Thief."

The elf gave the half-goblin a quick, boob-engulfing hug. "You can dodge him, my little man."

Although the thief didn't have the most hit points, he had the best chance to Dodge. It was a combination of the Coordination and Luck Stats. Snix didn't understand the stated reason for the logic, but it made sense. If the thief could evade the dire boar's attack, it gave the rest of the adventuring party a chance to attack unfettered.

The half-goblin used a forearm to rub sweat from his brow, and took a few steps back while the rest of the party spread to the left and right.

The big warrior, standing several strides from the gnome said to him, "We didn't hire the NPC to fight. Should've let the thief try to recruit the NPC to join the fight. He's got the Diplomacy Skill."

The gnome shrugged. "Sorry."

"You're cute and cuddly," the big warrior said. "Gets you favorable Reactions from NPCs, but that don't count when it comes to life or death."

"Got it."

The big warrior stuck his sword point first into the ground. He took up his bow and nocked an arrow. "Just hope your buddy the thief doesn't get gored."

Chapter 10

The dire boar came trotting directly toward the thief. Frothing saliva and dust from the road covered its curved tusks. The creature was half again the size of the adventuring party's largest ox.

The half-goblin began stomping his feet, waving his arms and shouting at the boar. "Hey, runt! Your momma's so ugly, she visited a haunted house and came out with a job application."

The big warrior loosed an arrow, then asked the gnome, "You share a mom with that boar?" All the party except the half goblin was kneeling and hunched down several feet from the road.

"Ha, ha," the gnome said, sarcastically.

The arrow arced down and struck the boar. The arrowhead hit at a bad angle and deflected off the tough skin.

The half-goblin thief picked up a rock and hurled it at the hog. The rock hit the boar's snout. The thief started yelling again, waving his cutlass. With his other hand he picked up a wadded garment. "Your momma's so fat, she *almost* fits into Kalgore's mom's nightgown."

Focused on the animated and loud half-goblin, the foul-tempered creature lowered its snout and picked up speed. The half-goblin thrust forward his left fist, holding the garment and uttered some sort of magical trigger words.

Nothing happened, at least not that Snix could see.

When the charging boar closed to within ten feet the half-goblin threw the garment at his foe's face. As the elf's cloak billowed open the thief dove and rolled to his left. The boar thrust its curved tusks at the cloak, catching it. It slowed, shook its head, then pinned the cloak with a foot and tore it in half with a tusk before tossing the distraction aside.

That gave the party time to attack. The big warrior gave up on his bow and ran forward with sword and shield. He hacked deeply into the boar's left flank. The gnome similarly attacked, slamming his cudgel against the creature's ribs to little effect.

Attacking the beast from its right, the druid drove in a deep thrust with his spear, and the elf loosed her Mystic Missile.

The boar bellowed a guttural growl as its eyes fixated on the elf. Before the party could attack again, the creature charged. The elf, wielding only a rapier, sensed her peril. She turned and ran.

The dire boar was fast, but the elf's swift speed left her only at a slight disadvantage. Her long strides over rocks and through grass left her party falling behind, but not the dire boar.

Her blue jay familiar dove, jeer calling at the boar's face. The bird pecked at its eye and flapped away.

The boar wasn't distracted.

When the dire boar closed the distance between itself and its target to less than a few feet, the elf cut right. Unable to change direction so quickly, the boar cocked his head to the right. As its momentum carried it past, the beast managed to clip the elf in the calf. The single tusk dug in deep. Neck and shoulder muscles twitched, jerking the boar's massive head and snout upward, sending the female cartwheeling in the air. She hit the ground hard, shoulder first.

Lying on her stomach, the elf didn't move. Snix spotted the gash ripped through her pants. Blood spouted from a wound torn in her calf, just above her boot.

The homunculus watched as the boar turned just in time for the druid's hurled spear to strike. The steel tip bit deep into shoulder muscle before striking bone. The boar snorted and bellowed in anger, and charged the four remaining party members. The blue jay dove down with wild abandon. Screeching, it landed on the charging boar's face and began pecking at its eye.

Snix took the opportunity to land next to the elf. Looking up to see the boar wasn't returning, he used one of his sharp claws to slice a piece of fabric from the elf's blouse. He wrapped it around the calf, just above the wound, pulled tight and knotted it. The blood flow slowed.

About forty yards away, the big warrior stood with shield ready and sword held high, shouting, "C'mon, ya ugly bastard!" The boar came right at him as the druid, half-goblin and gnome angled in from the side.

The druid hacked with his short sword, but the blade didn't bite into flesh. The gnome swung his cudgel and connected with a rear leg. The half-goblin leapt onto the boar's haunches. With his left hand, he grabbed ahold of coarse bristles, and with his right he hacked down with his cutlass.

The warrior sidestepped and hacked down with his sword. Steel blade bit into snout.

He took the brunt of the boar's charge on his shield. Still the collision sent the big warrior flying ten feet through the air. He landed hard, but quickly rolled, trying to get to his feet.

The boar came on. From his knees, the big warrior raised his shield and stabbed forward with his sword. The tip found flesh. The boar bowled over and trampled the fighter.

Kalgore didn't get back up.

Snix tore another strip of cloth and tied it over the wound, slowing the bleeding to a trickle. She'd live, if either the gnome or druid used even the least bit of healing magic on her. Seeing the bird abandon its attack on the boar reminded the homunculus of the problem the familiar caused. Taking advantage of the moment, the homunculus reached beneath the torn blouse, along the spine and hooked his claws into the clasps that held the elf's supportive garment in place and twisted.

That done, he retreated—just in time. The blue jay landed next to his master, and warbled piteously. The female driver abandoned the wagon and ran toward the fallen elf.

The half-goblin somehow clung to the boar's back, hacking and stabbing with his cutlass.

Like it'd done before, when Snix had bitten the dire boar, the creature dropped and rolled.

The half-goblin leapt clear and landed on his feet, like an apprentice acrobat.

Before the boar managed to regain its feet, the druid charged in and attacked with his sword, followed by the gnome. Both blade and wood struck. Neither successful attack was severe, but the cumulative number of wounds were adding up.

The boar got to its feet and turned toward the gnome. The short-statured healer lifted his shield and backpedaled slowly. "That's all you got, bacon bits?" He stopped and cocked back his cudgel. "Come on, Porky

Pig!"

Snix didn't understand the riled gnome's taunts. He flew high above the battle. It was moving away from the big warrior, so the homunculus flew toward him.

The female driver stopped to check the elf. Satisfied she wasn't going to die immediately, the driver stalked forward, angrily shaking her war hammer.

After the gnome went down, Snix wondered if the three remaining could finish the wounded dire boar.

The gnome didn't have time for a third taunt. The dire boar charged. The gnome stood his ground but, at the last second, threw his shield at the boar before diving forward. The boar tipped his snout up to deflect the shield, allowing the gnome to slip beneath the tusks as the creature charged past.

Somehow, the gnome emerged unscathed.

The druid and the half-goblin, however, each got in a side attack with their blades.

The boar spun about and eyed his three attackers. He didn't notice the female driver racing up from behind.

The half-goblin shouted, "Way to go, Captain America."

The gnome replied, "Back at ya, Spider Man."

The boar snorted and bellowed, and lowered his head. Instead of waiting for the creature to pick a target, the remaining adventurers and their driver closed on the boar in unison and attacked. It was brutal and bloody, but the dire boar finally collapsed under the weight of its many wounds.

The half-goblin came away with a nasty gore-wound to the abdomen, and the druid had an apparent dislocated shoulder. But all were alive and standing.

Before the dust settled, the druid said, "Jax, go heal Marigold." Without waiting to see if the gnome had listened, he rushed to the downed big warrior.

Snix retreated from the unconscious human.

"She's gotta be okay," the half-goblin said in a strained voice.

The driver called to the sprinting gnome, who was closely followed by the half-goblin, clutching his wounded abdomen. "She's alive. Her leg wound's tied off."

The druid knelt over the warrior and began the words to a spell. He placed his hands on the big warrior's forehead. After the big warrior regained consciousness, he started to sit up, groaned, and fell back.

The druid said to the driver, who was standing next to the two adventurers, "Your assistance ending the fight is much appreciated."

She smiled. "I should've been in the fight from the start."

"That assertion is in error," the druid said. "Your primary function is to drive and care for the oxen and horse. You performed your primary responsibility admirably."

Before she could respond, the druid said, "My remaining two Cure Minor Wounds Spells will not completely heal Kalgore. Please retrieve the wagon so that he may ride in the back."

"What about the gnome?" Kalgore asked, as the druid prepared to cast a second spell.

"You are cognizant of Marigold's severe injury?"

The big warrior nodded.

"In addition, during the final rounds of combat, Gurk received a severe abdominal wound from a dire boar tusk. I calculate that it will require two of Jax's Minor Heal Draw Spells, and most of his available hit points to heal both Marigold and Gurk."

The blue jay familiar stood next to its master's head. She lay sprawled on her stomach, face to the side with locks of black hair covering it.

The gnome didn't take a half moment to examine the elf, or even brush the hair from her face, or turn her over. He sat down next to her, took her limp hand and began his spell. A moment later, the gnome sat with his jaw clenched in pain.

A healer's spellcraft drew wounds upon himself, leaving the recipient of the effort healed and free of whatever wounds or injuries that healer took on. Then the healer's internal magical ability to heal wounds and injuries kicked in. Often a healer would be left only partially healed—until spell energy was renewed.

Even as the bruise damage taken on by the gnome faded and the leg wound began to close, the elf awoke. She took a deep breath and then pushed herself from the ground.

"Oh," she said, as she shifted to a sitting position. She smiled at the gnome, who grimaced, and waved a shaky hand at her.

The half-goblin remained standing, a hand and forearm pressed against his midsection, blood seeping past his fingers. "Hey, Marigold," he said in a strained voice. "We won."

The elf looked past the half-goblin, taking in the dead dire boar lying on its side, and the druid kneeling down next to the big warrior lying prone. The female driver stood over them.

Marigold took a deep breath. "We did win, didn't we."

The blue jay landed on his master's shoulder. "Petie," the elf said, staring into her familiar's eyes. Snix figured they were communicating mentally, like he did with his master.

The elf shrugged her shoulders, then felt for the shoulder straps of her supportive undergarment. "Petie," she said, "which of these two pervs unhooked my bra?"

The gnome stared at the elf, mouth agape.

The half-goblin sat down next to the gnome. "Jax was busy throwing his shield around like Captain America, and I was busy getting close and friendly with a dire boar tusk."

"What about that jerk, Kalgore?"

"He was fighting too," the gnome said. "He got gored twice and trampled right after you got hurt."

The elf slapped a hand on the dry ground. "Why do I miss everything good?" The motion reinforced the fact that her undergarment was unhooked.

The half-goblin groaned and signaled for the gnome to heal him. "Probably came undone while performing your Olympic areal train wreck maneuver," he said.

The big warrior lay back. After receiving the druid's two remaining curing spells, he said, "At least you didn't waste one of those on that stupid bird."

"I assure you," the druid said, "I endeavor never to waste a spell."

"If you say so," the big warrior said, sitting up with assistance from the druid. "Do me a favor."

"Of course."

"I want you and the thief to cut out those big 'ol tusks for trophies."

"That is reasonable." He stood, then offered the big warrior a hand up. The female driver offered a hand as well.

The druid asked, "Anything else?"

"Yeah." The warrior looked around for his sword and shield. "Being a druid, you know where to harvest bacon from on a dire boar. Right?"

Chapter 11

After travelling a short distance, the adventuring party considered building a fire to cook some of the bacon cut from the dire boar. Cautioned by the druid, the party's leader, about bringing notice to themselves, they settled for cooking a small portion over the gnome's magical candle.

Each got a bite, including the driver. The big warrior, nursing his wounds in the back of the wagon, got two.

The next morning there was excitement. At first Snix thought it was due to the warrior being healed by the gnome. Rather, it was about a dream the big warrior had. It earned comments about being third rank, having eight more hit points after his Constitution Bonus was added, and that he took the Tracking Skill. The party engaged in a social ritual of slapping hands, called "high five." Even the elf and the big warrior engaged in the ritual with genuine smiles.

The gnome mentioned how he hoped to be next, soon.

The only one not understanding was the female driver. She watched the celebration, not the least bit curious as to what it all meant. Snix's master had overheard conversations by customers that visited the pawnshop, usually adventurers, that mentioned ranks and hit points, and even something referred to as armor class rating. Higslaff believed it correlated to the amount of protection that various sorts of armor, shields and enchanted items offered while engaged in combat.

The adventuring party soon returned to their normal

routine, and verbal snipes.

In the late afternoon, the big warrior rode Four Banger back toward the wagon. The druid was driving, with the elf on the bench seat to his left and the gnome to his right. In the back of the wagon, the driver rested, casually watching the road. The half-goblin thief was frustrated, attempting to repair the undergarment that Snix, himself, had damaged.

Snix's garment sabotage proved distracting to the elf, and her familiar. The bird flew mostly behind the party, watching for danger, keeping away from the big warrior who scouted ahead.

The elf caught the big warrior watching her large chest bounce as the wagon wheels rolled across a rut in the road.

"Come back to get an eyeful of jiggle joy?" the elf asked, sitting up strait and jutting her breasts out.

The big warrior sneered, then grinned. "Jumbo jiggle joy." Then his face scrunched up. "Would be more entertaining without a steel codpiece."

Keeping pace on horseback with the wagon, next to the gnome, the warrior said to the druid, "There's a couple wagons heading this way, about a half-hour off."

"Did you observe any other item of concern?"

"Nah, Lysine." Then the warrior asked the elf. "Your bird see anything trailing us?"

She closed her eyes for a moment. While she did so, the gnome handed the warrior a canteen. After taking a long drink, he stoppered it and tossed it back. "Thanks, gnome."

The elf's eyes snapped open. "Petie doesn't see anything, except a big porcupine."

"Right," the big warrior said, and rode back ahead at a canter. His head looking left and then right as he advanced.

When he was out of earshot, the elf asked the druid, "What's a codpiece?"

"A metallic piece of armor that protects a male warrior's genitals from injury."

"Oh," she said, "like a cup?" She shrugged. "My high school boyfriend played catcher." She looked ahead, at the warrior. "Serves him right."

"Marigold," the druid said, "I believe you have yet to fully comprehend the significance of a nineteen point one Appearance Score."

"If it means stares galore and ogling at these." She cupped her breasts, lifted them and turned toward the druid.

The elf being significantly taller than the druid, he was forced to lean right to avoid contact with his cheek and shoulder. "I have observed the effect of such a high attribute and the additional attention your generous feminine attributes attract." Despite the awkward angle, he shrugged. "I must admit that, despite my constant effort, I have observed your appearance, and your generous assets, in a way that is unbecoming of a gentleman. For that, I apologize."

Looking away, the gnome said, "Me too, Marigold."

From inside the wagon, the half-goblin added, "Me too, dudette."

She leaned back and threw her hands up in

frustration. "It wouldn't be so bad if my clothes didn't get destroyed all the time. This isn't the first time my bra's been destroyed. Luckily I brought along another blouse, but my cloak is destroyed—again."

The druid cleared his throat. "In my experience, RPG adventures tend to acquire recurring patterns. Those patterns are influenced by the Game Moderator, the world he created, and the players. To a lesser extent, the RPG, including its rules, and even artwork, have an impact."

He glanced at the elf, who looked at him skeptically. "An eighteen is the normal maximum," he said.

After a moment of the wagon trundling over the road, the druid spoke some more. "The GM is a dastardly individual, who is both meddling and vindictive. I believe your creation of a character that not only has an astoundingly high Appearance Score, but physical traits that are also outside the norm, may be influencing the trend you described."

"I can't help it I rolled four sixes."

"And you opted to play an elf, a race which is given an automatic plus one to Appearance."

"I wanted to play an elf, like in *Lord of the Rings*. I didn't know I was going to *be* one."

"The abnormal height and..." The druid paused. "Other extremely generous anatomical proportion you recorded on your character sheet."

She interrupted the druid. "That was Gurk's fault."

"Not completely," the gnome said. "You did it to get reaction content for your sociology paper."

From within the wagon, the half-goblin said, "That's right. You tell her, Jax."

The elf looked away, down at the passing ground in

frustration. "So, you think that jerk GM that stuck us in this stupid game world is influencing what happens, from where he is. Our world?"

The druid shook his head and shrugged. "Kalgore and I have discussed the possibility."

"You never told us," the gnome said.

"If we came to a determination that the GM is influencing events, it would have been shared. Dare I say that you and Gurk and Marigold do not share details of all conversations you have amongst yourselves. But, if something pertinent to our survival, or effort to return to our world, were realized, that you would share it?"

"Yeah," the gnome said. "That makes sense."

"So, what you're saying is, that I should expect my clothes to get destroyed, like, pretty much every adventure we go on?"

"There may be a way to mitigate the effect of such occurrences." The druid offered a crooked smile. "Minor Mending is a first rank Magic User Spell. It can be used to repair damaged articles of clothing."

A broad smile spread across the elf's face. She reached over and hugged the druid.

After being momentarily half-smothered, the druid remarked. "It is fortunate that I do not wear a metallic codpiece."

Both elf and druid laughed.

The gnome asked, "You'd select Mending during an adventure, instead of Slumber or Mystic Missile?"

The ill-timed question shattered the momentary mirth.

From within the wagon, the half-goblin said, "I'm gonna need to use one of your blouse's buttons to fix your bra, Marigold."

"What?" she asked.

"Yeah," he said. "I cut a slit where the wire hooks were, and reinforced it with thread so it'll hold. I need a small button to finish it."

She huffed and tore a button from her blouse and threw it back into the wagon, at the half-goblin. "There. You happy?"

"Dude, I wasn't talking about *that* button. I wanted to use one from your torn-up blouse."

"What?" the elf said.

"I didn't wanna go digging in your pack without permission."

"Oh," the elf said. "I'm sorry, my little man."

The half-goblin brought the button back up and offered it to the elf.

A wicked grin crossed her face. "Keep it, Gurk." She looked down and adjusted her blouse to reveal a little more cleavage as they trundled along. Gazing ahead at the big warrior, she asked the druid, "How much codpiece discomfort do you think some *generous* jumbo jiggle joy will cause?"

CHAPTER 12

The next morning the elf sat to the left of the female driver as she controlled the oxen. The half-goblin sat on the right. The druid rode the horse, scouting ahead. The big warrior was asleep in the wagon and the gnome watched out the back. The familiar stayed close and was beginning to cause trouble again, forcing Snix to latch onto the bottom of the wagon.

During the night, Snix had snuck into the wagon and removed all of the buttons from the blouse he'd torn up to make bandages for the elf's bleeding leg.

The road was damp from last evening's rain, so the ride was slower, but less rough.

The elf asked, "When do you think we'll reach Shorn Spearhead?"

"Several hours after noon," the female driver said.

"Sucks. I'll probably have to hide back in the wagon, so I don't draw undue attention."

"We'll get you another cloak," the half-goblin said. "Or maybe a straw hat, to at least hide your face."

"It gets old."

"And you think being a half-goblin doesn't?"

"But, you chose…"

"None of us chose to be here, Marigold."

A few moments of silence passed, except for the wagon creaks and the oxen breathing and plodding. The female driver broke the silence.

"Miss Marigold, you consider your beauty a curse." There was a pause. Snix suspected the driver stared earnestly up at elf as she said, "Would you rather have a face like this?"

Snix thought of the driver's round, weather-beaten face framing a crooked nose. She wasn't a beauty among humans, but would be more acceptable than the half-goblin. Snix didn't see why humans didn't care for half-goblins.

"Sometimes," the elf said.

More silence, until the elf said, "Oh, hey, Lilac."

"Yes," the driver said.

"I never thanked you for tying my leg wound off." To Snix, it sounded like she reached down and patted the spot where the dire boar wounded her. "Gurk said I might've continued losing hit po—I mean kept bleeding, and maybe died if you hadn't."

"Miss Marigold, I didn't tie off your wound. I thought it was one of your friends that did it."

"Really?" the elf said.

"So, you didn't do it?" the half-goblin asked. "And none of us did it—we didn't have time with fighting the dire boar."

The elf asked, "Then who did?"

Snix imagined the driver and half-goblin shrugging their shoulders. He wondered if they'd figure out none of them had bandaged the bleeding elf.

"You didn't do it, and didn't see anybody do it?" the half-goblin asked.

The driver said, "I was driving the wagon away."

"And nobody else did it," the half-goblin said. "And nobody saw it done."

"We already know that, Gurk." The elf sounded frustrated.

"I know, Marigold. I'm just trying to think it through."

"Brownies are known to do good deeds," the female

driver said. "When nobody is watching."

"Yeah," the half-goblin said, "but they live near villages and hamlets, not out in the middle of nowhere." He snapped his fingers. "What about a fairy?"

"Fairies don't live near swamps," the elf said. "Not nasty ones like the Dark Heart Swamp."

"Okay, dudette, so what's your explanation?"

"How should I know? You know more about *Monsters, Maces and Magic* than I do."

"Then why shoot down my idea? After all that's happened with you, a fairy makes the most sense."

"I bet Lysine will know," the elf said.

An hour later, after the druid and the gnome and big warrior joined in the discussion, they decided upon a fairy using her camouflage ability. Especially after the shadow they saw a couple days back. In case it wasn't a fairy, Petie and the druid, with his enchanted crystal, would have to pay more attention.

Chapter 13

A wooden palisade protected the town of Shorn Spearhead. The wagon passed by clusters of farm cottages surrounded by fields growing wheat, beans, potatoes and turnips along the way.

The driver turned the oxen-pulled wagon off the main road and onto a gravel road that passed through an apple orchard. The town sat off the main road by a quarter of a mile. The palisade was tall enough that an ogre couldn't see over, but could probably climb, if the guards atop didn't use their crossbows to stop such a venture.

The main gate stood open without a guard. Getting closer, the deep meadow grass nearer the town was being harvested by men swinging scythes.

The big warrior rode in ahead of the wagon. The female driver sat on the bench seat with the gnome and druid. The elf and the half-goblin sat in the wagon, concealed from view by the canvas covering.

Inside the palisade the town looked like a patchwork of buildings, nothing uniform. Wood, brick, stone, in all combinations. Some structures started as stone and had been added to using brick or wood, or both. Others appeared to have originated with wood, and expanded through use of stone or brick.

A main street bisected the town, with its shops and other buildings lining each side. A street, if it could be called that, left a space between the outer facing shops and building fronts, and the palisade. Short boxy structures, mostly residences, were tucked against the interior palisade wall. Those that didn't have stout doors set with a small shuttered window had sturdy, metal-reinforced doors closed with rusted padlocks. Those were for storage.

The druid directed the driver to follow Kalgore. He led them to a stable where they could leave the wagon and have their oxen and horse looked after.

"As discussed," the druid continued, "Kalgore and Lilac will deal with the stables. Gurk and I will seek a buyer for the bricks, while Marigold and Jax secure two rooms for the party. Lilac, I trust you will remain at the stables?"

Snix figured she must have nodded agreement, because the druid continued, "We will then meet at the inn to finalize our plan."

"I'm going to get a cloak before going to the inn," Marigold said.

"Understood, but do not unnecessarily delay reserving rooms, as the day is coming to an end. Shorn Spearhead does not offer an abundance of accommodations."

Since he wanted to know where the party would be located overnight, Snix followed the elf and gnome.

The Aviary Inn was built of cut stone and included three floors. The outer wall was a honeycomb of small alcoves. Nearly all of the cavities provided a nook for a bird nest. That was going to be a problem for Snix. But it might also keep the blue jay away. It was to be expected in a town run by a former adventurer that went by the name, Birdman.

Behind the inn stood Kolger's Tavern, or conversely the inn was located behind the tavern. They were connected by a tunnel passage between basements.

Snix had once entered the Aviary Inn with his master, hiding inside a sack. During that same journey, he'd found purchase outside one of the tavern's shuttered windows that offered a limited view and hearing. It wouldn't be bad, depending upon where the party might sit.

"After I get a new outfit," the elf said, "I want one of those tub baths, even if they only offer lye soap." She mumbled about replacing buttons Kalgore refused to admit stealing. The one replacing her bra's broken hooks had popped off and gotten lost.

The gnome had to trot alongside the elf to keep up. "I remember the trading shop that has cloaks and pants and stuff," he said. "I doubt they'll have a complete outfit that'll fit."

The elf stopped, catching the gnome by surprise. He came to a halt a few steps past her.

Shorn Spearhead wasn't a large town. Nor did it boast a large population, but there were a number of workers and residents going about their business. The elf's abnormal height drew enough attention. Her bouncing chest, long black hair, and the fact that she was an elf did more than turn heads. Being paired with a gnome, also an uncommon race, was an additional factor. His short stature, just over four feet tall, and her being over six and a half feet, reminded Snix of a human mother and a young child. But human children didn't have facial hair that extended into sideburns.

Stopping on the side of the hard-packed road, outside of a baker's shop wasn't helping with anonymity. A few birds flying past seemed to take notice of Snix in the air above the gnome and elf. Their surprised chirps and whistles were thankfully ignored, due to the two adventurers' disagreement.

The elf rested her hands on her hips. "What's that supposed to mean, Jax?"

"Well," he said, drawing the word out. As he did, he stepped further off the road and next to the bakery's door. He signaled for the elf to follow.

She looked around, hand going to the missing button on her blouse. She suddenly became self-conscious of the attention she was drawing.

"Forget it," she said, and marched toward the textile shop just up the street.

The gnome ran to catch up. "It's just that you're so tall, and a woman. So a tall guy's stuff probably won't fit right."

"Just my luck. You're probably right."

A guard with a shield and mace stood outside the entrance to Kolger's Tavern. He wasn't a problem for Snix. The man was alert, but his focus remained on people walking the streets or approaching the tavern. Snix slowly crawled along the wall, keeping to the shadow formed by the porch's overhanging roof. Despite sundown, the heat of the day was still on the town, and the window shutters were all open.

Like the door, the wooden shutters were reinforced with metal. If they'd been closed, it would've proven a serious challenge. Sneaking in when a door swung open, with a guard, and the individuals going in or out would've made it risky. As it was, the homunculus climbed in the window from the top at a snail's pace to avoid drawing notice.

Once inside he clung to the wall, near the plank ceiling, in the shadow of a support beam. The tavern hadn't changed since he was in it last. Few places changed, unless visited by some form of destruction, followed by rebuilding. Even then, change was rare. His master's business was rebuilt to match what had been destroyed by fire. The furniture and layout of his master's office, and residence, never changed. Snix attributed it to most humans being creatures that clung to familiarity and habit.

The same eight polished pine tables, with six to eight chairs around them, stood in the same places. There were smaller tables as well as a birchwood bar with high stools. A combination of lanterns and several weak Light Spells lit the tavern. The same odors of stale human sweat, spilled beer and coal smoke filled the room.

This time, in addition to the usual chatter, arguments, and laughter, a minstrel sat on a high, corner stool and played tunes on his fiddle.

It was early in the evening, and a bustling business meant most of the tables were taken. Snix easily spotted the elf and gnome sitting at a small table along the wall, near the bar. A few seconds later he spotted the other party members. The big warrior sat on a stool at the bar, his back to the elf and dwarf. He ate an apple while holding a tankard with his other hand. He grumbled and cursed to himself, probably to discourage someone from sitting next to him.

The half-goblin and druid were seated at a table near the entrance. They were drinking as well. The druid did most of the talking, discussing various types of trees and their value as firewood. The half-goblin nodded, appearing to pay attention, but his eyes regularly surveyed the room and the people in it.

The druid did as well, but he mainly watched people enter and exit the tavern.

As a predetermined signal to those bringing the item his master wanted in trade, a wand that could detect foes, the gnome wore a black top hat similar to the type his master preferred to wear himself. This one had a brown band and blue feather. The party had arrived in the first day of a four-day window to meet and make the transaction.

The gnome wore the hat well, probably better than any of the other party members could. He looked around in anxious glances, only half paying attention to the elf, who complained about the bath she'd taken, and how she didn't like the ugly brown color of the hooded cloak she'd bought. And none of the buttons matched her blouse's buttons.

The half-goblin had managed to sew a new one onto her bra.

The blue jay familiar was resting on the sill of the first room they'd rented for the night, occasionally flitting over to the second rented room's sill.

After less than an hour of the gnome nursing his second ale and the elf ordering her third cup of wine, a thin, dour-looking man approached their table. He was balding with a wispy mustache and wore dusty traveling clothes. He was armed with a matching pair of daggers.

"It *is* you." The thin man grinned broadly and reached out to pat the gnome on the back, but stopped. "Ah, you don't recall."

"Maybe," the gnome replied.

"Well, it's easy for me to recognize a gnome. You're so few and we humans breed like rabbits—or rats, depending how you shorter folk tend to characterize us." The thin man cocked his head as he appraised the elf. "A beautiful elven dining partner."

The thin man cleared his throat, then said to the gnome, "Last time we met, you were with a cleric of Athena." He winked at the elf. "Although she couldn't hold a candle to your elven radiance."

The elf moved a hand through her dark wavy hair. A wide smile spread across her face. "Why, thank you so much."

The thin man gestured at the gnome. "It must be the hat. My great uncle had one just like that, and he always seemed to attract the company of beautiful women."

Snix recognized the code signals, mentioning "the hat" and a "great uncle."

"I recall now," the gnome said, awkwardly. "We met in…Spot on the Plains." He fumbled at adjusting the hat on his head. "Why don't you join us—if you don't mind, Marigold?"

Spot on the Plains, a crossroads town to the north, was the return code to solidify the connection for the transaction.

"Ahh, Marigold, a fitting name for such a beauty."

Snix was impressed how the man's dourness evaporated in the presence of the elf. Or he was accustomed to displaying many faces, and playing many roles.

"Yes, please do," the elf said. "My companion, Jax, hasn't shared much about where he's travelled."

"I can spare but a short time, for a drink together," the thin man said to the elf. "My friends call me Dusty." Then, taking a chair, he said to the gnome, "You're buying, my friend." He laughed. "You owe me, remember?"

"Of course," the gnome said, grumbling. "How could I forget?"

The thin man spoke mainly to the elf. When his eyes weren't sneaking peaks at her cleavage, his attention was on the room, or what he could see without turning his head too far.

"Well," he said, after draining his mug of beer, "I have a rendezvous with a surly man in the plum orchard west of town before sunrise." He pushed his mug to the center of the table. "Plum wine. I don't care for it, but there are those who do."

"I had plum wine at a Japanese restaurant once," the elf shared. "On the sweet side, but not bad."

The thin man glanced at her with a blank expression. "You elves," he said, scratching his head. "Gotta go." He nodded once to the elf. "Grand to meet you, Marigold."

"It was nice to make your acquaintance, Dusty."

Then he extended a hand to the gnome. "Good seeing you again, Jax."

The gnome slid off his chair and they shook hands.

"You too, Dusty."

The thin man looked around and made his way out the front door. After he did so, the gnome said, "You aren't old enough to order wine."

The elf leaned forward and whispered, "I used a Fake

ID."

The elf giggled and the gnome snickered at some sort of inside joke, because Snix didn't know what "Japanese" was, nor did he know there was an age requirement for elves, who were near immortal, to drink wine. But he did gather that a "Fake ID" was something that made it otherwise permissible and, by the whispering, not available to most elves. Although, there were no other elves in the establishment that might overhear.

While the pair was laughing, the half-goblin thief got up and left the tavern. Snix was about to follow him when a human female approached the gnome and elf at their table. She had blue eyes and shoulder-length blond hair. She wasn't particularly tall, and wore a mail shirt and skirt, with breastplate. Although polished and well-maintained, scars of combat covered both the front and back plate.

"Might I join you?" she asked in a polite, sincere tone. A hand rested on the pommel of her arming sword. She'd been at the bar, two empty seats away from the party's big warrior.

The gnome and elf shared a quick glance before the gnome gestured to the seat Dusty recently occupied. "Sure," he said.

When she was seated, the gnome said, "I'm Jax." He pointed to his friend. "She's Marigold."

"I'm Elisha Justine Woolwine."

Something about the blond female threw the pair off for second. It appeared to be her necklace with a bronze pendant in the shape of a cross.

"Marigold, Jax," the blond female said. "I am sorry to interrupt, but I had a question that I believe Marigold can answer." She made eye contact with the elf. "If you'd be so kind?"

Skepticism fell across the elf's face. "I'd like to know, how you know, that I know, the answer to what you want to know."

Dimples showed as the blond female smiled. "I know that you know what I want to know, because of who you are."

The elf's eyes went wide and she looked at the cross again. "Because I'm from the same world as you?"

The gnome said, "You got here by playing *Monsters, Maces and Magic* too?"

The blond female cocked her head. "I arrived in Shorn Spearhead by caravan, working as a guard. I'm a sentinel." Her eyes held sincerity. "I have encountered what everyone would call monsters, but I did not taunt or play with them. I dispatched them as quickly as my sword skills allowed. I have not trained in the use of a mace." She thought for a second. "I am not knowledgeable about enchantments, and would not delve into their use with any sense of play."

Both the gnome and elf appeared to deflate, at least emotionally.

The gnome gestured with his hands. "Ignore what I said. It was…"

"A silly joke that only a gnome would get," the elf said, reaching over and resting a hand on the sentinel's forearm. "He asks me things like that all the time."

The gnome scrunched up his nose. "I do not."

The sentinel gently but firmly reached with her left hand and lifted the elf's hand from her forearm.

The elf retracted her hand. "I'm sorry. That was so rude of me. I—we don't even know each other."

"No," the sentinel said. "I intruded while you were enjoying a private conversation." She gestured to her sword's pommel. "It is just that I prefer my sword arm remain unbound in any way."

"Oh, that makes sense." The elf sat up straight. "We've gotten off on the wrong foot. Let's start over. Elisha Justine Woolwine, I'm Marigold, and this is my friend, Jax."

"I am pleased to meet you," the sentinel said with a smile. "Thank you for sharing your table with me."

"Would you like a drink?" the gnome asked. "Seems I'm the one buying tonight."

The sentinel shook her head, causing her fine blond hair to sway. "Not tonight, I am afraid but, I promise, should we meet again, I will owe you each a drink, if you'll answer my question."

The elf's eyebrows shot up. "Okay, ask away."

The sentinel looked up to the left, in thought, then said, "An elf once said to me: *Heeya ma dorm'e e garmue hom.*"

The elf cocked her head slightly. "He really said that to you?"

Before the sentinel could respond, the elf said, "Ohh." She started to look around the tavern, but stopped. "It was a compliment, Elisha. He approved of your outfit."

The sentinel laughed. "Well, I guess that *is* a compliment, coming from a handsome elf to a human."

"He'd be an idiot not to," the elf magic user said. "You're very attractive. Don't you agree, Jax?"

The gnome nodded vigorously. "He'd be a complete dolt."

The sentinel smiled again, dimples showing as she

blushed. "That is very kind, and I thank you both for the compliment. And for answering my question, Marigold. Someday I may learn the elven tongue."

"Gnomish would be better," Jax said, "then you'll be able to translate this: *No re sol cha fleen.*"

The sentinel repeated the gnome's phrase then said, "I may come across another gnome first."

The gnome, despite his tea-colored skin, blushed as he worked to suppress a smile.

"I must depart," the sentinel said, standing up from her seat.

The elf and gnome stood in response.

The gnome tipped his top hat and bowed slightly. "I look forward to that drink. And so does Marigold."

The sentinel returned to the bar and paid her tab, and then left.

When she was gone the elf ordered another cup of wine and scooted her seat closer to the gnome's. She whispered. "In about fifteen minutes, me and you need to be someplace."

The elf looked around and sipped her wine, leaving the gnome to scratch his sideburns.

Snix only disturbed two owls while trailing the gnome and elf. He spotted the druid following his two party members, doing his best to remain unobserved. He wasn't too bad at it, but couldn't match a trained thief. A town setting wasn't where a druid felt most comfortable, although it seemed that this druid didn't mind so much.

The elf informed the gnome that what Elisha really said in elven was: "Meet me next to the textile shop."

The two party members hadn't communicated with the druid about their destination, and seemed unaware he was trailing them.

The elf asked the gnome, what he'd said to Elisha in gnomish? He declined to answer, seemingly embarrassed.

It wasn't yet late in the evening, and a few people still travelled up and down the town's streets. Weak Light Spells sporadically located on the sides of buildings or cast upon scattered posts offered enough light for humans to find their way. The guards stuck mostly to the palisade walkways.

The gnome and elf walked past the front of the textile shop, looking around carefully. They spotted someone in the narrow space between it and the candlemaker's. It was the sentinel. She'd donned a brown knit hat, and had stuffed her blond hair up beneath it.

The sentinel stepped out and said, "Please follow."

The gnome hesitated, but the elf tugged him by the arm.

She led the two adventurers to one of the storage buildings tucked against the palisade. She withdrew a key from a pocket along the inside of her calf-high boots and unlocked the padlock.

The sentinel looked around. Satisfied that no one was paying attention, she ushered the gnome and elf inside. Following, she pulled the wooden door closed.

Snix found slits in the storage building's wall, just beneath the roof's overhang. Probably for ventilation.

The gnome held his everlast candle, providing a flickering glow among the crates that filled only half of the building's interior. The gnome and elf were listening to the blond female.

"Listening and observing was part of my training as a sentinel," she said. "The muscular warrior two seats away from me at the bar, and a dirty man with a scar through his eyebrow at a nearby table both listened in on your conversation with the man who introduced himself to you as Dusty."

The elf caught something in the sentinel's tone. "So his name isn't Dusty?"

At the same time the gnome accused, "You listened in on our conversation."

"No," the sentinel said to the gnome. "But by the way they leaned and tipped their heads, and ignored all else around them, it was apparent what they were attempting."

The gnome squinted one eye and stared up at the sentinel. "Then how do you know the man's name is Dusty—or he said it was his name?"

"I heard him introduce himself, before sitting down and your private conversation commenced."

The elf's right hand moved closer to her rapier's grip. "So, what *is* his name, if it isn't Dusty?"

The sentinel observed the elf's posture and hand position. "We travelled in the same caravan to Shorn Spearhead. We both worked as guards. I know him has Skart." She shrugged. "The different name provided to you caught my attention."

"Why should we believe anything you're telling us?" The elf shook her head.

"Skart—or Dusty, served many nights on guard duty with me. He carried a spear, along with his two daggers. The way he handled the spear showed minimal, possibly no training in that particular weapon's use. He blended in well, kept from getting noticed. He watched members of the caravan more closely than he did for intruders."

"So?" the elf asked.

"Yeah, so?" mimicked the gnome.

"I served as a paladin's squire, for Marie, Champion of the Downtrodden. Like her, but in my own way, I strive to warn and ward those in danger."

Snix held back a hiss. He didn't like paladins. Neither did his master.

"So," the gnome said, "you think we're in danger."

"Of course we're in danger," the elf said to the gnome, exasperated. "Since we got stuck here, when haven't we been in danger?"

The gnome bit his lip. "We're supposed to meet Dust—Skart tomorr—"

The elf slapped her partner on the shoulder. "Shhh. Gurk and Lysine said we gotta keep things a secret."

"Keeping secrets is important." The sentinel smiled, making eye contact with the gnome. "Especially for your kind." Then she gazed up into the tall elf's eyes. "I suspected that you and Skart discussed something important. And two individuals, neither of which I believe are associated with Skart, were listening in. I recommend you plan accordingly."

The elf asked, "Why aren't you telling your buddy, Skart, instead of us?"

"You're a beautiful elven maiden and he's a cheerful gnome, a loyal companion."

"How do you know he's loyal?" the elf asked. "And they say beauty is only skin deep."

"She is kinda bitchy sometimes." The gnome flinched as the elf slapped him on the head.

"You sound just like Kalgore."

"Nuh uh." The gnome grinned. "He says you're bitchy *all* the time."

The elf rolled her eyes, then explained to the sentinel, "Kalgore is the big warrior at the bar."

The sentinel crossed her arms. "That leaves the man with the scar through his eyebrow. With all the dirt from travel on him, *he* should be named Dusty. Whatever your business, you need to watch for him."

The gnome stared at the floor and grumbled that sentinels probably get bonuses to Hearing, or Perception Rolls.

"That's only one person," the elf said, a sound of relief in her voice.

"And anybody he tells," the gnome said. He looked up at the sentinel. "If he was listening, and if he heard anything."

The sentinel tilted her head back and forth in equivocation. A few strands of blond hair slipped out from beneath her knit cap. "I believe you have the measure of it." She moved toward the door. "I wish, you Marigold and Jax, and your companions Gurk, Lysine and Kalgore, luck tomorrow."

The gnome bit his lip and glanced up at his companion.

"Skart, too," the blond female continued. "By my estimation, he is a thief."

"You don't trust thieves." The elf's statement wasn't a question.

"As much as I trust a fox to wander past a hen house."

The gnome scratched a sideburn. "Unless the fox has someone that'll kick his butt if he's been told to do something else." He picked up his everlast candle and moved toward the door.

"That is probably true." The sentinel prepared to open the door. Before she did she shot an accusatory eye down at the gnome. Then she pointed to her breastplate and whispered to the elf, "In case no one has told you, Marigold, you're missing a button."

The gnome slapped his hand over his mouth, stifling laughter. Obviously, his gnomish ears had heard.

The elf said to the sentinel, "Thank you, Elisha Justine. I already know." Then she slapped the gnome on the head. "You, not a word."

Chapter 14

Rather than divide into two rooms at the Aviary Inn as planned, the adventuring party crowded into one room, with one person remaining awake in rotation. Neither the elf, nor the gnome slept well, even though he seemed comfortable sleeping beneath the elf's cot. Although the elf didn't sleep, her trance or meditation or whatever elves she did, seemed disturbed. In contrast the half-goblin and big warrior snored away. The druid was up early for the final watch. Using the gnome's enchanted candle, he spent part of the time writing in his small leather-bound book.

Snix found that when the elf's familiar was close, the druid's enchanted crystal did not identify a second magical creature. Fortunately, the blue jay remained close and sound asleep on the windowsill of their room at the Aviary Inn.

During the night Snix hadn't spent much time looking in the window from the top. Listening sufficed. Communication with his master told the homunculus that, if he detected an impending attack or plan to steal the rubies, to find a way to bring the danger to the adventurers' attention.

He'd heard the adventuring party's plan, formed after the gnome and elf reported their encounter with the sentinel. The half-goblin thief had lost the trail of Dusty—or Skart, just as the druid lost track of the gnome and elf when they ducked into the storage building.

Snix wasn't overly impressed with the party's victory over the brigands along the road to Shorn Spearhead. Their plan to exchange payment for the Wand of Foe

Detection sounded reasonable. The execution of that plan would tell the tale.

If they failed, Snix hoped they'd fight hard. It'd make his task of retrieving the wand from the victors much easier.

Even before the gates opened, the half-goblin thief snuck out by climbing down the palisade. His job was to find a place to hide and observe the exchange. And the blue jay familiar was already in the plum tree orchard.

"Explain to me again," the elf asked, "why I left my bra on the wagon with Lilac?"

"Because," the big warrior said, trailing behind the group in the pre-sunrise darkness, "your little pal thief said it might cause a distraction—give us an edge."

"You were pretty quick to agree," she replied. "Like all I'm good for is some sort of sex object."

"Beautiful women clad in revealing attire is a motif of the *Monsters, Maces and Magic* game world." The druid rested his spear's shaft on his left shoulder as they walked. "I agree, it is a questionable underlying world structure. However, we must endeavor to leverage every advantage toward our survival."

"I think it would be a bigger distraction if Kalgore the Courageous wore a Speedo."

"I got the muscles to pull it off," Kalgore said. "But being the party's main combat machine requires a good armor class."

The elf laughed ironically and hefted her chest.

"*Lucky* I have the package to pull it off."

The gnome snickered and shook his head.

The big warrior asked, "What's so funny, gnome?"

"Nothing, Kalgore." Despite saying that, the gnome worked hard to stifle his laughter.

"Yeah," the elf said. "What's so funny?"

The gnome adjusted the shield on his back and hustled to keep up with the druid's pace. He said to the elf, "I'll tell ya later."

Balling his right fist, the warrior said, "Spill it now, gnome."

The gnome became somber. "Really, it's nothing."

"Jax, I concur with Marigold and Kalgore." The druid shifted his spear to his right shoulder while observing the road behind them. "Divulging a humorous thought or observation may alleviate accumulated stress. It may also eliminate potential penalties to Perception and Diplomacy rolls during the imminent transaction we have been hired to complete."

"Okay," the gnome said, his shoulders hunched while holding his hand over his mouth, suppressing another laugh. He took a deep breath. "I agree, Marigold showing off her super big asset package might be a distraction."

"Ginormous package," the elf interjected.

The gnome nodded agreement. "Ginormous." He took another deep breath. "But it'd be nothing compared to a Speedo-wearing warrior showcasing his super-tiny package."

Chapter 15

Resting on a branch and blending into the foliage of a nearby plum tree, Snix remained confused. He was sure the big warrior would pound the little gnome into a bloody mass. Instead he patted the gnome on the back—really hard—and told him, "That was a good one, gnome."

Maybe the big warrior was not smart enough to make the connection that there was an implied insult—at least his experience in observing male humans suggested it was an insult. Or, maybe what the gnome said *was* funny. All four adventurers laughed.

Now they stood in the darkness near the center of the grove, their backs to each other, several paces apart, looking outward. The half-goblin thief sat motionless on a nearby tree's bough, near its trunk. Foliage from branches laden with ripening plums hung down and obscured his outline. The blue jay familiar flitted from tree to tree, occasionally flapping up above the canopy to search for anyone approaching.

After ten minutes the elf whispered, "Petie sees someone coming. Three people." She closed her eyes. "One of them is Skart."

"Dusty," the big warrior reminded her. "Think of him as Dusty, so if you gotta talk to him, you'll call him that."

"Right," she said, nervously. "Thanks."

Their plan was for the druid to do the talking. The elf would speak up to help smooth things over, if needed. The warrior was there as a show of muscle and intimidation. The gnome was to smile and look inoffensive, and put those they were dealing with at ease. And to watch their back.

"No problem," Kalgore said, adjusting his shield's strap across his forearm. "We don't wanna tip our hand about knowing anything more about him."

The druid attached two pouches to his belt. One contained worthless pebbles. The other held the rubies. He stepped the direction toward which Dusty approached. The elf moved to his left and the warrior to his right. The gnome took his place a half pace behind and to the elf's left.

The thin, once again dour man approached. His clothes remained covered with dirt from travel, although it was apparent he'd washed what hair remained on his balding head and had trimmed his wispy mustache. The result left it a little uneven, adding a slight slant to his face. He came only armed with his matching pair of daggers. No spear.

Two men flanked Dusty. Average looking humans, middle-aged, each wearing a mail shirt, heavy boots and carrying a spear. They weren't overly impressive, Snix thought. But a few spear thrusts could ruin any creature's day. The real reason they were there was to facilitate Dusty's escape, should things go wrong.

Through his observation, Snix knew the adventurers his master hired were there to trade for the wand in earnest. Dusty didn't know that. The thin man also didn't know that a half-goblin thief rested on a tree branch only ten yards away. The party successfully predicted the direction from which the thin man would approach.

Dusty and his men advanced through the rows of

plum trees, stopping when they were ten feet from the druid. The thin man noted the elf's and gnome's presence with a nod, as well as the big warrior's. A mild hint of recognition came over his face after his gaze momentarily rested on the big warrior. Then he started to look around.

"Let us proceed with the exchange," the druid said, "such that each party might be on their way without avoidable delay."

The thin man's left eyebrow quirked upward. "You appear to be in a hurry?"

"Indeed," the druid said. "We believe that someone overheard the arrangements for this meeting."

That caused both of the thin man's eyebrows to rise. "In that case then." He held out his left hand and one of the spearmen pulled a wand from a long pocket sewn into the heavy trousers along his thigh. He handed it to the thin man.

"This," the thin man said, "is the wand your boss desires. May I see the rubies?"

"A reasonable request," the druid said. He selected one of the pouches from his belt and poured the rubies onto the palm of his hand.

"How do I know that they aren't paste?"

"If it were our intention to cheat you with false gemstones, would that categorize us as foes?" The druid put the rubies back in the pouch and crossed his arms. "Utilize the wand's attribute to determine if we are foes."

The gnome was doing his job, looking around for danger. Despite the dim morning light, the eyes of the two men accompanying the wand-bearer were more interested in the elf than anything else.

Snix nearly hissed, giving himself away, when five

men and a large gray war dog suddenly appeared in the plum tree orchard, fifteen yards behind the thin man and his two spear-wielding guards.

Chapter 16

The new group appeared through use of a Transport Spell. Snix had never traveled using one, and knew it took a very experienced and skilled magic user to cast one. The gray-bearded magic user who'd cast it stood with a staff in his left hand, and wore clean blue robes. A silver belt held pouches and a dagger. It was clear the man had cast the spell and not completed the incantation through use of a scroll containing the spell.

A thief and cleric were the other two men of note. The cleric's unholy symbol, silver on black depicting a skull in front of a barred gate, hanging from a chain around his neck, identified him as a follower of Hades. His armor was scaled, as if it were made from the pelt of a black dragon, and his round shield bore a skull, as did the business end of his steel mace.

The thief, Snix could see, bore a jagged scar through his left eyebrow. His hairline was receding, but he still bore greasy curls. This leather armor spoke of years of use and the grip to his short sword showed it wasn't a showpiece.

The other two men were unremarkable humans, wearing helmets and mismatched scraps of armor. They each held a battle axe. One carried a round shield. The other's gauntleted hand held the spiked collar of a war dog. The trained attack animal was stocky with short, gray fur. Much of the torso's fur was covered by leather armor adorned with metal spikes.

Snix knew what war dogs could do. This canine was at least as big as the gnome. Its dark eyes and bared teeth made it look a lot more dangerous than the gnome.

Digestive juices gurgled in the homunculus's gut. The party his master hired wasn't up to confronting the new group. Even worse, if they could Transport Spell in, they would probably Transport Spell out, taking the wand with them. There'd be no way he could follow.

The druid and his party's wide-eyed gazes, directed past the thin thief's shoulder, caused the thief and his two spearmen to look over their shoulder. They did so just in time to hear the thief with the eyebrow scar say, "Lay down your weapons and you'll live."

The scarred thief's rote voice sounded like he was bored.

"Who are you?" the thin thief asked.

"Doesn't matter who I am. What matters is that you were foolish enough to work for that petty pawnshop owner." The scarred thief paused. "What's his name?"

The druid adjusted the grip of his spear, from its butt resting on the ground to a defensive position. "Feigning that you do not recollect a name is insulting. This encounter need not result in bloodshed on both sides."

"Three sides," the thin thief said, turning around to face the scarred thief and his party.

The two warriors in front of the scarred thief laughed at the druid's comment. A sinister grin crossed the Hades cleric's gaunt face. The magic user couldn't have looked more unimpressed.

The scarred thief pointed at the thin thief. "Don't you plan on going anywhere." Then he said to the druid, "You will either drop your weapons, and prepare to spend the rest of your life digging in a sulfur mine..." His gaze shifted toward the elf. "Except for you, my fair elf." His smile turned menacing. He gestured to the cleric on his right. "Or my friend will ensure your undead corpses dig." He sighed. "I've been told the latter method provides less productive digging, but that really isn't my concern."

"That threat concerns me greatly," a forceful female voice said.

The words came from the left of the druid and his party.

All heads turned to see the sentinel, her blond hair covered by a steel helmet, but the intense gaze of her blue eyes showed from within its protective shadow. Her right hand rested on the grip of her arming sword while her left arm bore a kite shield adorned with a stylized painting of an eagle.

The thin thief took the distraction as an opportunity to make a run for it, sprinting to his right, away from the confrontation. The magic user, anticipating such an action, released a spell. A second later a blob of gel appeared around the fleeing thief, enveloping him like a mouse drowning inside a bowl of clear molasses. An Enveloping Gel Spell. Snix had seen one before. The thin thief was doomed to suffocation.

The thin thief's entrapment drew everyone's attention—except for the druid and the big warrior. The druid's hurled spear travelled in a shallow arc at the magic user. At the same time, the big warrior charged, shield raised and sword in hand.

An instant later, the full battle commenced.

CHAPTER 17

The druid's spear bit into the gray-bearded magic user's thigh before the big warrior closed half the distance between himself and the magic user. Despite this, the magic user got off another spell—a Major Lightning Spell. Pointing his index and middle finger, he directed the forked bolt of energy at the charging big warrior and one of the thin-thief's spearmen. The electric blast blew the latter ten feet through the air, leaving the man's chest with a charred hole the size of a fist. Rings of his mail armor were melted into his flesh and a sickly, steaming smoke from boiling blood rose from the downed man's mortal wound.

The big warrior, however, appeared immune to the energy of the fork directed at him, as well as the thunderous boom that accompanied the magical attack. He charged forward as if nothing more than a throw pillow had been tossed at him.

Everyone, even the magic user's allies, were temporarily deafened by the echoing thunder crack. The druid, closest to the bolt's path—with the dead spearman in front of him—staggered back a step, partially stunned.

The second of the entrapped thief's spearmen held his spear at the ready, facing the attacking party, but didn't advance.

The axe-wielding warrior with a shield moved to interpose himself between the big warrior and the magic user. He was knocked aside by the half-goblin thief who'd leapt from the tree branch onto his back. His cutlass *clanked* against the warrior's helmet as they both hit the ground hard.

The Hades cleric completed a spell—an Arrest Movement Spell, by its effect. Both the druid and the hesitant spearman stopped abruptly, frozen in place. The sentinel, preparing to engage the other axe-wielding warrior and his released war dog, slowed in her movement for a fraction of a second, but managed to throw off the spell's effect.

The sentinel, intent on attacking the Hades cleric, had to fight her way through the axe-wielding warrior and his trained attack dog. She commenced to doing that. She inflicted a draw cut to the warrior's leg—only a minor wound. The dog got around behind her and locked its jaws on her calf. Its teeth didn't pierce the sturdy leather. Nevertheless, the attack hobbled her as the war dog attempted to drag her down.

The elf released a Slumber Spell. It succeeded in causing the war dog's jaws to release as the canine dropped into a deep sleep. As for the gnome, he'd lifted is shield and charged, his cudgel cocked back. He shouted at the scarred thief, "You're mine!"

The amused thief, with short sword in hand, gestured for the gnome to bring it on.

Snix left his hidden perch and flew through the branches of the trees, toward the entrapped thief. The man was doomed, flailing like a moth ensnared in a spider's web. Snix couldn't do anything to save him. But, once the man succumbed to suffocation, the homunculus might be able to somehow reach the wand. Or, if the enchanted gel vanished, he'd be on hand to snatch it before anyone noticed.

Snix spotted the blue jay sitting quietly in a tree, possibly considering the same. The bird just might be big enough to hold the wand in its clawed feet and fly with it. At least for a short distance. If it managed, Snix was confident he could wrest the wand from the familiar.

The big warrior reached the gray-bearded magic user and slashed mightily with his long sword. The magic user backed away, attempting to avoid the blow but failed. He staggered back, a deep gash across his chest showed through his blue robes as blood began to soak into the fabric. He retaliated with a Mystic Missile Spell. Six, blue-glowing orbs shot from his pointing index finger and slammed into the big warrior.

The spell attack didn't appear to be enough to kill the warrior. He just dropped his sword and collapsed, unconscious.

The half-goblin and the axe-wielding warrior separated and were now on their feet. The warrior had lost his shield, but he appeared more than a match for the thief and his cutlass. The thief backed away and hurled a dart from his bandoleer left-handed. The warrior ducked his head to the right and avoided its point.

The thief drew another and taunted the bigger man. "That's all you got, dude? My grandma's little toenail is tougher than you."

The warrior charged. The half-goblin backpedaled in retreat, toward Snix's position.

The gnome wasn't very fast on the charge. Maybe he'd slowed down, seeing the big warrior fall. He'd stopped shouting and mumbled instead, still closing with the waiting thief.

The sentinel continued exchanging blows with the axe-wielding warrior. He wasn't able to get past her guard, but neither was she able to land a decisive blow.

The Hades cleric was standing still, casting what must've been a complex spell. The elf disrupted the effort when her pink Mystic Missile hit him. The cleric glowered at the elf for a second, then seemed to realize the minimal effect of the spell—nothing like what his magic-using partner could cast. Annoyed far more than injured, he began another spell.

The gray-bearded magic user briefly examined his wound. Apparently confident that he wouldn't bleed out from it, he looked around and then cast another spell. Another Mystic Missile Spell erupted from his finger. This time the fist-sized blue spheres sped toward the sentinel.

The blond-haired woman staggered back, enduring the onslaught of blue missiles. Unlike the big warrior, she didn't go down. But, like the gray-bearded magic user, she appeared severely injured.

The axe-wielding warrior stepped over his unconscious dog and pressed his advantage over the sentinel.

The elf drew her rapier and ran toward the half-goblin, still backpedaling from his foe. At the same time her familiar took to the air.

The scarred thief gestured again, awaiting the gnome's completed charge. The gnome slowed his charge to a trot, but kept closing. At the last moment, the gnome cut right. After several strides he dove toward the downed big warrior and rested a hand on his prone party member's forehead. He managed to complete the spell he'd been working on before the scarred thief knew what his opponent was doing.

The gnome fell unconscious the same instant the big warrior shook his head, sat up and looked around.

Before the scarred thief reached the gnome or warrior, the blue jay dove in, jeer calling and drove its beak deep into the back of the scarred thief's neck.

The gray-bearded magic user saw the big warrior grab his sword and climb back to his feet. Gripping his staff and backing toward the Hades cleric, he uttered another spell. A wad of stringy spider web the size of a fat groundhog appeared and shot from his extended hand. The big warrior ducked and rolled to the side, avoiding the expanding stringy glob. The Web Snare Spell continued expanding until its sticky strands engulfed the nearest plumb tree.

The half-goblin taunted his axe-wielding foe again. "Dude, your momma's so ugly, when she dances at the Blue Bugle, everyone throws coins so she'll keep her clothes on!"

That enraged the axe-wielding warrior. He saw that the half-goblin was backing toward the magical glob that'd smothered the life of the thin thief. Confident there was no escape, he rushed the taunting half-goblin. The thief stood to take the attack and then shifted left. But he kept one leg stretched across the charging warrior's path, tripping him. The man stumbled forward and into the gooey, gelatinous mass.

The warrior managed to slow his momentum so that his face and hands penetrated the gel only a few inches. But, before he could pull himself free, the half-goblin brought down a devastating cutlass strike against his exposed back.

The Hades cleric completed his spell. The warrior with the melted armor and hole in his chest climbed to his feet as a zombie. The evil cleric pointed and commanded, "Kill the elf."

Hearing the cleric's command, the elf, who was running to help the half-goblin, turned to see the undead creature. Her gaze flitted between the zombie and her rapier and back. As the creature reached out and began shambling toward her, she said, "Oh, double crap!" turned and ran. "I hate those things."

Snix, having seen the elf's fleetness of foot, knew the zombie wouldn't be able to catch her.

The gray-bearded magic user, being chased by the big warrior reached the Hades cleric's side. He grabbed the cleric's hand and completed a spell. They were gone, an instant before the big warrior managed to thrust his long sword's tip into that spot.

The scarred thief, while cocking back a dagger, preparing to throw it at the blue jay familiar, saw his two partners Transport away. It took a half second for him to decide the tables had turned against him. Almost as swiftly as the elf, he dashed to escape the fight.

Unfortunately for the scarred thief, he discounted the gnome, probably thinking he remained unconscious, or wasn't a threat. The gnome was on the ground. The healer leapt forward like a stumpy toad and latched on to the fleeing thief's right ankle.

Snix saw the half-goblin slash deeply into the axe-wielding warrior's hamstring. The man had extracted his face but hadn't freed his hands from the enchanted gelatinous blob. The big warrior, cussing away, ran to help the faltering sentinel in her fight against her axe-wielding foe. The elf was out of sight, and the druid and spearman were still held immobile by enchantment.

The homunculus remembered that the scarred thief held a grudge against his master. He couldn't let such a man get away. Deciding to take a risk, the homunculus folded his wings and dove. He landed next to the scarred thief, who was lying on his side, kicking at the gnome's head with his boot, trying to get his smaller foe to let go.

The scarred thief sensed something nearby, but not swiftly enough. Snix darted in and bit the man's cheek before leaping away. He drew blood while leaving behind some venom in the small wound.

The homunculus got away and into the air before the half-goblin thief arrived to assist his party member. Already, the scarred thief's struggle to escape became lackadaisical. His attempt to stab the gnome with his dagger lacked focused strength. The sleep-inducing venom was working.

The big warrior cut the remaining axe-wielder down from behind.

The half-goblin wound up and let go with a vicious kick. His leather boot connected with the downed man's crotch. Snix lacked those anatomical features of a human, but he was aware of the disabling results. The man grunted while his eyes rolled up in his head. A half breath later, he was out.

The big warrior turned around and asked, "Thief, where's Marigold?"

Standing over the prone scarred thief, the half-goblin said, "That evil cleric dude animated one of delivery dude's henchmen into a zombie. Then he ordered it to 'kill the elf.' She took off faster than a greyhound chasing a rabbit."

"You heard him, gnome," the big warrior said. "The thief called Marigold a dog."

"I did not!"

"Which way did she go?" the sentinel asked, sword held ready. "She may need our assistance."

"No way a zombie'll catch her," the half-goblin said. "Petie'll let us know if she's in trouble."

"Petie?" the sentinel asked.

"That's her familiar," the half-goblin explained. "He began patting down the scarred thief and going through his pockets. "Jax, go find something to tie this dude up with."

The sentinel appeared confused at the lack of concern. "What about your associate?" She gestured toward the unmoving druid.

"Gotta be an Arrest Movement Spell cast by that evil cleric guy," the half-goblin said. "The one you took issue with."

The gnome trotted over to the sentinel. His nose was bleeding, and one of his eyes was turning black from getting kicked in the face by the scarred thief. "Thanks, Elisha Justine. Without you—"

"Hey, gnome," the big warrior said. "The thief asked you to get something to tie that guy up."

The injured sentinel smiled down at the gnome, dimples showing. With minor difficulty she sheathed her sword.

"You're name's Elisha?" The big warrior firmly gripped her arm. "I'm Kalgore. Let me help you over to that tree." He gestured to a nearby one. "You can sit down there." As they walked, he continued, saying, "Once Lysine gets unfrozen, he'll be able to do a little curing. He's a druid."

After the big warrior helped the sentinel down to the ground so she could lean back against the plum tree's trunk, she asked. "How did you survive that magic user's bolt of lightning?"

"Got a fulgurite that negates them."

She nodded once, seeming to understand. "Are you sure Marigold does not need assistance?"

"Nah," the big warrior said. "Here comes her bird. She'll be right behind him." He winked an eye at the sentinel and whispered. "Watch. Soon as she gets here she'll start bitching about something."

The sentinel raised an eyebrow. "If she is not in danger, maybe you could find something to make into a muzzle and tie it around that war hound's snout. Tie him to a tree so he doesn't run off?"

"Good idea," he said and turned. "Gnome, bring me that asshole thief's belt so I can make it into a muzzle for that war dog."

The gnome was busy tying the thief's wrists behind his back using the thief's own boot laces. "Do it yourself. I'm busy."

The big warrior turned to say something to the half-goblin, but the thief was poking around at the gelatinous glob with his cutlass.

"Dude that cast this was tough," the half goblin said. "We gotta get that wand and get outta here."

"Yeah, someone's bound to come see what caused that thunder boom," the big warrior agreed. He looked up into the tree next to him. "Hey, bird, where's Marigold?"

A moment later the female elf ran into the small clearing.

"Where's the zombie?" the half-goblin asked. He stared at her, eyes wide.

"I outran it, and circled back around," she said. Her familiar landed on her shoulder. "Think it'll, like, bother anyone or try to kill them?"

"Not unless they're an elf," the big warrior said,

tugging the belt off thief the gnome had just finished binding up. "A freakishly tall one, with a chest half falling out of her shirt."

The elf rolled her eyes and adjusted her blouse. "I lost another button running from that creepy zombie thing." She threw her hands up in the air. "Why do they always gotta come after me?"

"See, Kalgore," the gnome said. "Marigold taking Running Skill was pretty smart after all."

The big warrior ignored the gnome and grinned at the resting sentinel, as if to say, "See, what'd I tell ya?" Then the big warrior went over and buckled the belt over the dog's snout and began searching the nearby dead axe-wielding warrior. "Marigold, get your bird to fly up and see if anyone's coming." He pointed toward the immobile spearman. "Then watch that guy."

He gestured toward the druid. "Gnome, Lysine's coming out of it. Tell him to get over to Elisha and cast a few cures while me and the thief gather the rest of the loot. We gotta get moving."

"Yeah," the half-goblin said. "And we're taking this dude, too." He kicked the bound thief. "Bet Higslaff'll pay us pretty good for capturing him."

Chapter 18

The adventuring party gathered together a short distance from the wagon. They'd pulled off of the road less than a mile from Shorn Spearhead. Some farmers were in the fields. They were too busy weeding with hoes to pay attention to the stopped travelers.

The female driver remained with the oxen, and the spearman, the henchman of the thief that died in the magically summoned gelatinous glob, sat in the wagon, keeping an eye on the bound, gagged and blindfolded scarred thief. Next to the thief rested a pile of armor and weapons scavenged from the battle.

The sentinel, partially healed of her wounds, stood a few steps from the huddled group, keeping watch.

Snix thought the party leader's concern was legitimate. He'd already made mental contact with his master, informing him of the success, and the capture of the scarred thief. His master was very pleased, but concerned about the party's ability to get the man back to Three Hills City. If they did, wonderful. If they didn't, it remained Snix's job to secure the Wand of Foe Detection.

Snix hid behind a pile of horse manure. It'd been dumped in the narrow strip of weeds between the road and the bean field. He had to be careful. The sentinel was more alert than the entire party put together. If she accompanied the party back to Three Hills City, the chances of him remaining unnoticed weren't good.

"We are unable to renew our spells until sunrise," the druid said. My suspicion is that the magic user is of Black Alignment, and will be able to renew his Transport

Spells after sunset."

"His spells are way better than mine," the elf said.

"Don't matter much," the half goblin said, "Either way, we're screwed."

The half-goblin kicked at a dandelion, then tipped his head up, staring at the sky in thought. "Magic user dude cast two Transport Spells. Means he's at least tenth rank. And I bet his evil cleric buddy is tough too."

"Even if we buy a set of horses with the rubies," the big warrior said, "and drive them to death, it's still four days to Three Hills City."

The half-goblin nodded. "More than enough time to recruit more guys and set up an ambush."

"Do we have to stay on the road?" the gnome asked. "Can't we go into the swamp and throw them off?"

The elf, wearing her new cloak, stared down at the gnome in disbelief. "Ewww, I hate that place."

"The swamp ain't exactly a safe place," the big warrior said. "It's a bad idea. Plus, we'll lose out on selling the armor and weapons for gold."

"Yeah," the half-goblin said. "That magic user guy might be able to find us in the swamp anyway. With a crystal ball or an Enchanted Search Spell."

The big warrior said, "Enchanted Search is fifth rank, thief. Would take away one of this Transport Spells."

"He probably used that to bip in on us in the first place," the half-goblin countered.

"Kalgore and Gurk, your observations have merit. Yet we should not dismiss Jax's suggestion just yet."

The gnome sighed. "I'd rather get ambushed on the road than in the swamp."

The elf threw up her arms in frustration. "Can't we

just let him go, and they'll leave us alone?"

The big warrior and half-goblin simultaneously said, "No."

"Events in an RPG generally are not resolved in that fashion," the druid said. "In this instance, our party will likely be considered middle-men, and not held responsible." He held up a finger, forestalling what the elf might say. "Our remaining a target of retribution, once the individual in question is turned over to another interested party, becomes a remote possibility. Until that comes to pass, we remain in danger."

The gnome said, "You're saying NPCs don't hold a grudge?"

The druid shook his head. "On the contrary, NPCs often do. However, most NPCs are unlikely to pursue actions related to that grudge unless precipitated by an outside influence."

"Like Creepy GM Dude," the half-goblin said.

The sentinel stepped closer to the huddled group. "Might I offer an option?"

The big warrior looked up from the group. "Sure."

"I am acquainted with Major Disaster, and he owes me a favor."

"We've heard of that dude," the half-goblin said. "He's a warrior, so he wouldn't have spells, like a Transport."

"That is true, my friend, Gurk. But he does have friends, and I believe one is capable of performing the spell that you seek."

"That'd be cool," the half-goblin replied. "Is it that big of a favor owed?"

She shook her head. "I imagine it will cost you the rubies Lysine carries in his pouch."

"Your willingness to utilize an owed favor on our behalf is appreciated." The druid's hand went to the gem-holding pouch tied to his belt. "The acquaintance of your associate, Major Disaster, would not have a problem casting a Transport Spell upon us, and an individual bound and gagged?"

"Major Disaster knows a lot of people." Her normally happy face frowned in disapproval. "If the man I am thinking of is still in town, he won't have a problem with it."

The guards on Shorn Spearhead's palisade didn't appear to notice or, if they did, care that the party in their wagon had returned. The sentinel directed them to a limestone structure, a two-story residence, with a guard seated in the shade of a small maple tree.

After the sentinel inquired if Major Disaster was in, the guard directed her to the stables, where Major Disaster was having his favorite mount re-shod.

Snix heard the half-goblin whisper an explanation to the gnome that introductions to an NPC from another NPC happened all the time in games, but that you had to really trust the first NPC. That told Snix they trusted the sentinel. That made sense, although he didn't know why she showed up in the plum orchard in the first place, let alone inform the party—complete strangers—of their conversation in a bar being overheard. It sounded like something a paladin might do.

Major Disaster's name was misleading, unless it was

referring to him causing other people's disasters. He had straight dark hair pulled back from a widow's peak on his forehead. His dark, deep-set eyes held little mirth. His breastplate and pauldrons were etched with stylistic dragons. The long sword on his hip radiated an enchantment that caused the juices in the homunculus's stomach to grow cold. It was a subtle magic that creatures of a non-magical nature might not pick up on. The elf must have felt something, as she appeared more standoffish than usual during the sentinel's introduction and when the druid spoke with the sturdy warrior.

After getting directions to a private residence where the spellcaster in question was staying, along with a scribbled note from Major Disaster and a complicated code phrase, that turned out to be a name, the sentinel returned to the wagon.

The muscular warrior stayed with the wagon, along with the female driver and the spearman named Gurse. The adventuring party was worried about keeping the bound and gagged thief lying under a tarp, and if anyone might try to rescue him.

The big warrior, standing outside the wagon, looking mean, deterred curiosity. Not as much as Major Disaster would, Snix believed.

The two-story apartment building was constructed of bricks and limestone. It had narrow windows whose shutters stood open. Oddly, none of the many birds inhabiting the town were perched on the apartment. Snix didn't bother wondering why, being thankful that their absence made his job of remaining unobserved easier.

The two half-goblin guards lounging in front of the door to the apartment appeared intimidating in a menacing way. Both stood up straight and eyed the party as it approached. One lifted his short bow and nocked an arrow. The other curled his narrow fingers around the grip of his scimitar, his wiry arm posed to unscabbard it.

"Halt," the scimitar half-goblin said, his yellow eyes roaming up and down the tall elf. "You hidin' another gnome under that cloak?"

The short bow half-goblin snickered, causing the tip of his ready arrow to bounce up and down. Both of the guards' leather armor showed signs of multiple combats and repair.

"My cloak, and what's under it are none of your business," the elf said.

"Will be when I shoot you there. Either you'll squeal or whatever's under there will."

The party's half-goblin thief said to the elf, "He's just tryin' to yank your chain." Then he said to the scimitar guard, "Dude, we're here to see if the guy you're guarding is interested in earning some coin."

The half-goblin thief took a step closer. The short bow guard drawing back the bowstring didn't seem to bother the thief as he said, just above a whisper, "A lotta coin, dude."

The druid rested a hand on the half-goblin thief's shoulder and drew him back. "I bear a brief writ of introduction." He proffered the page torn from his leather-bound book, written on by Major Disaster.

The scimitar half-goblin snatched it and squinted at the writing. A left eyebrow arched, and he showed it to the short bow half-goblin.

"Watch 'em," the scimitar half-goblin said. He turned and knocked twice on the thick wooden door. After a long moment, the door opened a crack. The scimitar half-goblin pushed his way in and shoved the door closed.

The short bow half-goblin stood and watched. After a moment he lowered his bow. He sat back down on his stool. "You all stand there and don't go nowhere."

"Of course," the druid said. "Otherwise we might squander our opportunity to meet with the individual you guard."

After several minutes, the half-goblin thief looked around and said to the seated guard, "Dude, I'm never able to get good guard gigs like this." He gave a thumbs up. "Good job."

The half-goblin guard grinned, then said to the elf, "What *do* you got under that cloak?"

"Wouldn't—," the elf began to snap back until the gnome stomped his heavy boot down on hers. She grunted and stuck her tongue out at the gnome. "Wouldn't want to be accused of distracting you from your work," she said, then offered an almost sincere smile.

The heavy door opened and the scimitar guard stuck his head out. "The guy with the paper and the elf woman can come in. You other guys gotta wait out here." A wicked grin showed his pointed teeth. "Oh, and you can't bring in no weapons, and no cloaks neither."

The elf handed her rapier to the gnome and the druid gave his short sword to the half-goblin thief. They started to step forward.

"No cloak, so you can't be hiding nothing under it."

"Whatever," the elf said. She unclasped the main hook, removed the garment and dropped it into the gnome's waiting arms.

The short bow half-goblin's eyes went wide as he whistled.

"Keep your hands to yourself," the elf warned, balling her right hand into a fist, "or those snarly teeth will've done their last whistling."

Snix left his hiding spot on the front-facing wall near the roof and moved around back. He thought there was a pair of narrow windows in the back. He hoped they weren't shuttered closed. And that the druid wouldn't be near one of them. It also reminded Snix he had to be wary of any familiars the magic user inside might have.

Snix managed to situate himself above the window and peek in. A sky full of clouds blocked the sun so no shadow would betray his presence.

The room was rather dark. An old human—very old human—sat at a table in the middle of the sparse room, facing the window. His chair was padded, and papers, rolled-up scrolls, and thick leather-bound tomes filled the long table. A flickering candle sat at each end of the table and a lit lantern hung from a hook in the ceiling.

The old man's head was nearly bald, except for scattered strands of white hair. He wore heavy black robes and had a gray knit shawl draped over his shoulders. Skin clung to his face and bony hands like it'd been there for centuries, all covered in dark age spots. His eyes, however, were alert as they followed a yellowing fingernail while it traced across what was written. Old didn't adequately describe the man. Ancient did.

While the homunculus waited for the elf and druid

to enter the room, he mentally contacted his master, telling him: *Two members of the party are about to see a very old magic user and try to convince him with your rubies to purchase a Transport Spell to take them and the thief they captured to Three Hills City.*

His master replied: < Magic users powerful enough to cast Transport Spells don't respond well to spies. Keep your distance and be careful. >

I will, boss.

Chapter 19

What appeared to be a cleaning girl escorted the druid and elf into the room. Cleaning girls normally don't have a stiletto's sheath sewn into their apron. She announced the guests. "Lysine and Marigold." Without waiting for a response, the maid stiffly turned and left.

The ancient magic user didn't look up from his reading to acknowledge the maid, or the druid and elf. He kept reading, his finger moving across the sheet, then down to the next line.

The druid took a relaxed stance, his hands behind his back, right hand holding the wrist of the left. The elf glanced around for a moment, then squinted her eyes, trying to see what the ancient magic user was reading.

"Careful," the ancient magic user said, his voice dry but surprisingly robust. "Gravity acting upon those voluminous breasts as you lean forward may cause you to topple. That would scatter my papers and candles. If that happens, I will kill you both." His finger returned to moving across the paper. "I will also kill the rest of your party." His grim smile matched is dark eyes, with sagging bags of skin under them. "When I get around to it."

The elf stood up straight. She started to say something, possibly an apology, but the druid shushed her.

After four or five minutes, the ancient magic user looked up from what he'd finished reading. "It is my understanding that Major Disaster believes your purpose is worth an interruption." His voice and demeanor suggested the ancient magic user did not agree.

"You are, and your purpose is?"

The druid cleared his throat. "Mr. Chisisuschugerganteramoski, I am Lysine, and this is Marigold." He gestured toward the elf. Snix was impressed that the druid recalled and sounded out the complex name with close proximity to Major Disaster's pronunciation.

"As your time is precious." The druid tipped his head forward in deference. "I shall be brief. I and my adventuring party desire to purchase from you the service of a Transport Spell to Three Hills City, for five party members and an individual that attempted to end our lives this morning." He slowly reached toward the pouch on his belt and untied it. "It is our understanding that you are capable of such a service. We would pay for this service with eight rubies."

"I am capable," the ancient magic user said. He pointed with a crooked finger at a clear spot on his table. "Place your proposed payment there."

While the druid emptied the pouch of rubies into his hand and delicately placed them on the table as directed, the elf asked, "Can you cast a Wish Spell?"

The question almost caused the druid to scatter the rubies onto the floor.

The ancient magic user's cackling laugh brought relief to the sudden tenseness in the druid's rigid shoulders.

"You are as beautiful as you are naive, my elfin maiden." The ancient magic user scrutinized her. "Such rare and arcane enchantments are not bandied about in pointless discussion." He gestured with a steady wave of his left hand at her chest. "Do so again, and I shall double the curse that some annoyed witch reasonably saw fit to visit upon you."

The surprised elf put a hand to her chest. "This isn't a—"

The druid slapped his hand over her mouth. "She is indeed, naive, and I apologize on her behalf."

The ancient magic user didn't acknowledge the druid's apology, or the perturbed elf. He brushed a gnarled finger over the rubies, examining them. "Leave the rubies and return with your party, and prisoner, to the foyer within the hour."

The druid deferentially said, "Relevant custom is to leave half to demonstrate earnest—"

Before he finished, something caught the ancient magic user's attention. Snix realized the ancient human eyes were fixed upon him.

A remarkably nimble flurry of hand gestures, accompanied by an incantation, left the homunculus unable to move. Try as he might, Snix couldn't retreat from the window. Nor could he flap his wings.

Startled by the magic user's sudden action, the druid took the elf's hand. "We shall return within the hour." He and the elf backed away.

Standing and waving a hand dismissively, the ancient magic user said, "Take your rubies and return, with them, as told. Now be gone."

The druid picked up the rubies before he and the elf departed the candle-lit study.

Chapter 20

Boss! I'm stuck. Can't move or get away.

<What happened?>

The ancient magic user must've cast an Arrest Monster Spell on me. He's walking over toward me. I'm stuck, hanging down, looking in the window.

<Didn't I tell you to keep your distan—forget that. Who is this ancient magic user? Tell me about him.>

Higslaff wanted to learn as much as he could before the magic user eliminated his homunculus. So, if it didn't turn out well, there'd be payback.

He's reaching up. He yanked me from the wall. The homunculus sent his thoughts quickly. Not from fright, but that he might run out of time. *He is staying in the first-floor apartment across the street from a dry-goods store. Two half-goblins guard the front and one is inside. The adventuring party is supposed to return in an hour. They are going to pay this ancient magic user with your rubies for a Transport Spell to Three Hills City.*

The human male is really old. Over one hundred winters. Almost no hair. Is an associate of Major Disaster. Chisisuschugerganteramoski is what they call him.

Higslaff repeated the name to himself.

Snix repeated it slowly. *Chis-is-us-chug-ger-ganter-amo-ski.*

He's looking me in the eyes.

That name sounded familiar. Not familiar in the way that the old magic user had been a customer, or associate of the guild, but he'd heard the name before. <What kind

of person is he?>

Snix knew his boss wanted to know how to deal with the man. *You'd call him evil. The type that kills. I think he is more powerful than Coleen Sammae. Sill Rochelle too.*

That made Higslaff think, and become more concerned. He and anyone he could recruit would have trouble taking on Sill Rochelle—unless they surprised her. This magic user detected and captured his homunculus. He would be difficult to surprise.

A few memories began to click about that name. The Winterlands, now ruled by the God Emperor. Higslaff went to the door and called down to his nephew, "Send Bomar up." The dwarf was his most loyal employee.

Boss, he has a dagger, with dark runes on the blade.

Higslaff sat down in his office chair, waiting for the pain and injury that would come when his homunculus was wounded...or slain.

The pawnshop owner felt pain from his elbow and along his forearm. First on the left side and then right.

Boss, he just sliced my wing membranes. He called for his half-goblin guard to bring the cage.

So, it would be negotiation. The sliced wings made it harder for his homunculus to get away.

Higslaff decided to take a chance. He didn't want his mind too closely bound with his homunculus while it was in the clutches of a powerful, evil, magic user. He concentrated and saw through his homunculus's eyes, for an instant, the ancient magic user's face.

That half second was all it took. Deep eyes that held less warmth than an abandoned doll's black button eyes. That magic user had lich written all over his soul's future. Why would the Birdman allow such a person into his town? He was supposed to be good, not evil. Not a paladin by any measure but...

Then a piece of the puzzle slipped into place. In one of the poems the bards sang about the conquest of the Winterlands, it was said that during a final battle the Psionic Knights had dismantled the Birdman's brain. In that song, or another about conquest of the Winterlands, Chi was named among other powerful magic users fighting the God Emperor's forces. He recalled once hearing "Chi" was short for Chisisuschugerganteramoski, a name which any bard would avoid in the singing of a tale.

Boss. The homunculus interrupted Higslaff's thoughts. *There's a big rat in the cage. The ancient magic user just obliterated it with a Mystic Missile Spell. He turned me to see it happen. Nine brown missiles, Boss. From one spell. There's not even a tuft of fur left in the cage.*

Higslaff knew that was a demonstration. Possibly a captured familiar killed. Snix wasn't frightened. He didn't respond to danger that way. He wasn't like a normal creature. That didn't mean Higslaff wasn't concerned.

Bomar entered the office. Higslaff picked up a pencil and wrote on a blank piece of paper: Get the 3 Healing Elixirs. If I drop, pour them down my throat. Send Vernie to get Josiah. He handed the note to the dwarf while maintaining communication with his homunculus.

<Keep reporting, Snix. How can the apartment be entered?>

The dwarf guard hurried out of the room and back down the stairs.

Two narrow windows in back. He is putting me in the cage, Boss. It is like a big birdcage, gold bars with runes. I

remain unable to mov—

Higslaff expected communication with his homunculus to be interrupted. That didn't mean he was happy about it.

The ancient man hadn't bothered to clear his table. Instead he ordered the half-goblin guard to close the shutters and then place the cage on a stool. It wasn't a stable platform but, from his seat, staring into the cage, the ancient magic user didn't appear concerned.

The half-goblin stood in front of the room's closed door with a short bow, arrow nocked and ready. He appeared eager to shoot something.

Snix found he could move. Nevertheless, he maintained his position on the cage's floor, in the center. He didn't want the cage to topple over with him in it. He didn't try to camouflage. It might work on the half-goblin guard, but he wasn't the one holding Snix captive.

"Foolish spy," the ancient magic user said. "Nod your head once if you comprehend what I am saying."

Snix saw no reason to not answer. He nodded once, maintaining eye contact with the magic user. The casual manner in which he killed the rat, the cage's former occupant, hinted he wouldn't hesitate to end Snix's existence.

"Excellent." The ancient magic user smiled. The smile did not reach his eyes. His teeth, for an old human, were white, like those of a youth.

He held the dagger he'd used to slice Snix's wing

membranes in front of the cage. "I will be casting a Telepathy Spell, so that we can converse. Actually, so that through you I can tell the one you serve what a fool he is, and inform him what he must do to regain your services."

He pointed the dagger at Snix. "If you attempt to escape, I will sever your wings, legs, and one arm. Both eyes. That will render you next to useless to your master, but keep you alive, so that I can periodically cut you, and cause the one you serve pain and injury whenever the fancy strikes me. And your master will remain unable to create a new homunculus.

"Do you understand?"

Snix nodded his reptilian head once.

"You will send my words, and my words only. And you will faithfully relay to me exactly what the foolish one you serve says. Do you understand?"

Even without flight, Snix thought that he could easily elude the half-goblin, and possibly the ancient magic user's dagger. But he couldn't expect to escape the ancient human's spellcraft. His magical ability to hide had shown itself to be inadequate against the ancient magic user's perception.

Snix nodded his head once.

"The fool you serve is aware that you have been captured and is prepared to converse?"

Snix thought about that question. He thought his master was ready, and thought he would converse, but his master didn't always do what Snix predicted. Rather than nod his head, he used a gesture humans used. He held out his hands, palms up and shrugged his shoulders.

The ancient magic user's wispy eyebrows drew together. His grip on the dagger tightened. The fake smile became a genuine, menacing sneer. "If the fool on the other end fails to respond, your ability to function in this existence…"

The ancient magic user did not finish his threat. Instead he opened the cage door and began to cast a spell.

Snix contacted his master. *Boss, the ancient magic user is going to cast a Telepathy Spell to speak to you through me. If you do not answer, he will cut off my wings, legs and one arm, destroy my eyes and keep me alive to occasionally cause you injury.*

Higslaff was surprised to hear from his homunculus so soon. There must be a deeper reason than simple expediency, if he could only figure it out.

His dwarf employee returned to the office. After dragging the big table across the floor, next to the desk, he placed the three crystal vials containing Healing Elixirs on it. He didn't say a word. Rather he silently awaited instructions.

Higslaff gestured for the dwarf to pull up a chair at the table. Then he replied to his homunculus. <I am prepared to talk.>

Higslaff didn't include: For as long as it is productive.

Chapter 21

[Who is the fool who sent this homunculus to spy on me?]

He heard the words through his homunculus's reptilian voice, but they had a harsher tone. That was interesting, and the question wasn't an unexpected way to start. <I am Higslaff. I own a pawnshop in Three Hills City. My homunculus was keeping track of an adventuring party I hired.>

[A commonplace merchant.] The dismissiveness came through, along with the words.

Higslaff didn't respond. There was no benefit in doing so.

Vernie opened the office door, letting Josiah the lay healer barber in. Higslaff penciled a quick note and slid it across the desk, toward the barber.

Josiah picked it up and read the message: Snix captured. Heal me of any injuries.

The barber saw damp bloodstains along the bottoms of the pawnshop owner's shirt sleeves. He shoved the note in a pocket, walked around the desk, and cast a Cure Minor Wounds Spell on his friend.

Bomar pointed at the three crystal vials and whispered, "Healing elixirs."

[Do you desire the release of your spy, foolish merchant?]

It was obvious the magic user was trying to goad him into an argument. To protest Snix being a spy, or himself being called foolish. In many aspects, including power and knowledge of magic, and holding of valuable cards in the negotiations, the ancient magic user held the advantage. Communications and years of coming out on top in a deal—or at least not losing his shirt—or life, was the pawnshop owner's advantage. One the overconfident magic user likely did not recognize.

<Yes, I do.>

No need to say more. Let the magic user ask the questions and set the initial price.

It would've been helpful to see the magic user's facial expressions, minor tells in body movements and posture. To hear his physical voice—his cadence, inflections, what he stressed—telepathy conveyed that, but it was being filtered through Snix's thoughts.

Higslaff shrugged to himself. The magic user was under the same limitations, possibly more. He wasn't familiar with Snix, and the homunculus's idiosyncrasies.

[Four days from this moment, foolish merchant. If you have not personally delivered sufficient bounty to purchase release of your spy, it shall remain my property. Finders, keepers, shall we say?]

Higslaff frowned. There wouldn't be a negotiation. At least not at this moment.

[Understood. I will be there to meet with you before the established time has elapsed.]

A sharp pain shot through Higslaff's shoulder. Blood appeared.

Bomar reached for one of the vials. Josiah signaled that he would take care of it. Two Minor Cure Spells later, Higslaff was without injury.

He dismissed the dwarf guard but signaled for his friend, Josiah to stay. He began jotting down notes and questions that needed answers. He also needed to let the guild know to expect an important prisoner within the hour. Josiah could do that.

CHAPTER 22

Josiah had returned to Higslaff's office to inform him that the guild was ready to receive the enemy guild member captured by the adventuring party. The plan was to deliver the individual to the barber shop because of its access to the underground tunnel system. A secondary plan was to take him to a small ship currently docked at the nearby port on the Snake Claw River.

Higslaff appreciated Josiah's concern for the situation with the ancient magic user. If Higslaff did nothing, his risk of death was small. But the potential for long-term aggravation and suffering was great. The pawnshop owner classified the ancient magic user as a Soul of Consequence, like himself. So, it was unlikely any gods that might take interest would favor one over the other.

The pawnshop owner held moderate wealth and resources. He needed to know more about this Chisisuschugerganteramoski to secure an agreeable settlement and Snix's release—unharmed. He was sure that gold wouldn't be a primary route to that end. He held a number of enchanted items in his business inventory. None of them would impress such a powerful spellcaster. Possibly the right balance of gold and magic—unless there was something else. Information or access? That route might resolve the current situation, but leave him in debt to, or under the thumb of, individuals he'd rather not be under.

While wandering down the storage room shelves, Vernie hustled up to him. "Uncle, the gnome named Jax and his friend, Gurk, are in the shop. They said you wanted to meet them when they got back to town."

"Send them up in a moment."

Higslaff went upstairs and put two of the vials holding Healing Elixirs in the top drawer of his desk. He kept one in his pocket. He shoved the table back to its normal spot and then sat back, clearing his mind. He didn't want to tip his hand, letting on that he knew about the captive, and the Transport back. Unless the ancient magic user had informed them about Snix. In that case it might've been a mistake not to reveal the presence of his homunculus.

Higslaff shook his head. The adventuring party certainly didn't know he had a homunculus. They certainly wouldn't be surprised that he might do something to keep track of them. He could use that to his advantage.

After Vernie let the pair of adventurers in, Higslaff stood and came around the desk, a friendly smile across his face, then frowned. "Only two? Is everyone in your party okay?"

"Yeah, we're all good, dude," the half-goblin thief, Gurk, said. They shook hands. He did the same with the gnome healer.

The young thief noticed the blood stains on Higslaff's sleeves but didn't say anything. He'd have to change shirts after the meeting.

"Please," the pawnshop owner said, gesturing to two of the chairs in front of his desk. "Have a seat." As he made his way around the desk, he asked, "You met with success?"

"Sure did, dude." The young thief's pointy-toothed grin was wider than Higslaff had ever seen.

The gnome pulled a wand from a leather scroll case

and placed it on the desk. "One Wand of Foe Detection."

"Plus," the young thief said, "we captured a thief that don't like you. Him and a tough magic user and a Hades cleric—and a couple of their henchmen—tried to take the wand." He frowned. "They killed the dude that brought the wand, though. We killed the henchmen, but the magic user Transport Spelled himself and the cleric away."

Higslaff picked up the wand and examined it, first by running his fingers across the delicate rune marks near its tip, and then using the goggles strapped to his hat. He then examined the wand using the jeweler's loupes attached to the goggles. Careful inspection showed it was enchanted, and the basics of what the runes represented.

"This appears to be the item you were contracted to retrieve." He set the item on the desk. "I did not expect you to return so soon. And with a captive."

The pawnshop owner leaned forward with his hands on his desk. "Although I will have Coleen Sammae cast an Ascertain Enchantment Spell, of course, I can gather the agreed upon gold for completing your mission."

Higslaff pursed his lips. "As to the captured thief of a rival guild?"

"Dude, the magic user that Transport Spelled them in, to try and steal your wand, killed the delivery guy in an Enveloping Gel Spell." The thief's nose scrunched up. "Like I said, he Transport Spelled away before getting it when Jax here healed Kalgore back up. Took off before him and the cleric got sliced up."

"They left the thief behind," the gnome healer said. "We thought they might try to come back and rescue him, so we bought a Transport Spell to get back here before they could."

If the individual you captured is indeed an operative from the rival guild causing trouble here in Three Hills City, you will certainly be rewarded." Higslaff leaned back in his chair. "That is out of my hands—although I will put you into contact with the right people. And put in a good word for your party.

"Can you get the individual to Josiah's barber shop?" Higslaff made eye contact with the young thief, knowing that he was aware of Josiah's access to the tunnel system there. "From there, the guild can shield him from the Transporting magic user, and work to determine who the fellow you captured is." Higslaff tipped back his hat's brim and raised an eyebrow. "Unless you want to do that yourself?"

"Nah, dude. We trust you guys on this. We can get him there, right away."

Higslaff knew they just wanted the man out of their hands.

"Tell you what," the pawnshop owner said. "You get the individual delivered, and tell Josiah anything you know, and then come back here for your payment—for the wand."

A notion struck Higslaff. A way he might learn a little more about the magic user holding his homunculus. "Then, your adventuring party can join me at the Blue Bugle tonight. Josiah too, if he wants." He rubbed his hands together. "I'll pay for entrance and the first two rounds of drinks."

The gnome nodded his head. The young thief said, "Sure thing, Higslaff. That'll be cool."

As soon as the two left, Higslaff wrote a note. He placed a gold and two silver coins on the paper and folded it. He sealed it with candle wax.

After the wax cooled the pawnshop owner called his nephew into his office. "Run this over to the Blue Bugle, and see that it gets to the bard scheduled there tonight."

The Blue Bugle was a center for entertainment in Three Hills City. It offered drinks, music, food and gambling. The entrance fee kept the poor out. Workers of moderate means could save and enjoy an evening a few times a year.

It was a wooden building with sturdy framing and actual windows. The front was single story and wide. The building extended back to become a three-story structure. The upper levels were restricted to higher-paying patrons, for gambling and private meals and entertainment. A large blue bugle was painted on the wall facing the narrow street where customers entered.

For some reason that Higslaff couldn't figure out, the busty elf took Josiah's arm as the group walked from his shop to the Bugle. His friend had a lucky streak a mile wide, and a grin that'd stay on his face for weeks to come. The pawnshop owner had to admit, there probably wasn't anyone as outright attractive as Marigold in the city. She was more than a head taller than Higslaff with a chest that, while not the largest in Three Hills City, was more shapely than any of its rivals.

Higslaff also knew Marigold was a tease. She might hold hands and listen to Josiah's jokes and pointless stories, but the barber would never wake up the next morning with her in his bed. Besides, unlike his friend,

Higslaff had a purpose. He needed to get a better feel for who the ancient magic user was.

He'd stopped by and asked Sill Rochelle to have a Transport Spell prepared for tomorrow, and that he'd need her to travel with him, and use a scroll with the same spell upon it—one she'd written—to return. That scroll cost him a small sack of gold. A magic user had to be accomplished, not only to cast the spell, but to create a scroll inscribed with it. Sill Rochelle was one of the few in Three Hills City that could. Other than for sale through his shop, at a profit, having the scroll on hand for an emergency, for himself or the guild, was also important.

Higslaff probably should have invited Sill Rochelle to join the group for the evening. He'd reserved one of the tables for eight. But, again, tonight he'd have been poor company for her, and she'd remember it.

The entire party had been Transported by the ancient magic user. But, from what Higslaff had learned through Snix—before his capture—Marigold, and the warrior druid, Lysine, were the ones that negotiated for the spell.

"So," Higslaff said, as the party made their way through the entrance. They were being led by one of the blue-jacketed doormen to their table. "The wagon and oxen are being driven back by Lilac, a guard that survived the fight, and a sentinel, that fought on your side?"

"That is correct," Lysine said. "They are to join a caravan south tomorrow. As compensation, they have been instructed to sell the weapons, armor and other gear obtained from the brigands defeated that Kalgore mentioned. And from those that attempted to forcefully obtain the item which you commissioned us to retrieve."

Higslaff thought that was far too generous. But adventurers, Favored Souls, were often like that. Also, there was a "tell" at the end of Lysine's statement. His eyes briefly looked down. They kept a couple more valuable items for their party. Generous, but not foolish.

The reserved table was on the first floor, round, with room for eight chairs, but with only seven placed. One had a padded cushion, for the gnome. Higslaff made sure he was seated between Lysine and Marigold. With the druid on his right, past him sat Kalgore and then Josiah. To the left, past Marigold, sat Jax and then Gurk.

Some disappointment rested on the barber's face. His seat wasn't next to the fair elven maiden, but the half-goblin thief to Josiah's right immediately engaged him in conversation.

The group's table was to the left of the stage, close enough that they'd be able to hear the bard, despite the background noise. The establishment was such that a quiet conversation wouldn't be overheard.

After ordering drinks and a light meal of mild cheese, broiled river bass and rye bread, Higslaff steered the conversation to the ancient magic user.

"Marigold, tell me about this old magic user that provided the Transport Spell."

She set down her goblet of wine with a sour look on her face. "A nasty old man," she said. "Not a pervert. Even with missing buttons, he hardly tried to stare down my blouse. Too old for that." She took another sip of wine. "That's probably why he's so mean."

"Mean?" Higslaff made sure to keep his eyes on the elf's beautiful face. "Did he mistreat you? Say inappropriate things?"

She shook her head, causing her waves of long hair to undulate across her shoulders. "Rude. Probably because everyone's afraid of him." She shrugged. "So old; he'll be dead soon. Bet nobody goes to his funeral."

Or undead, Higslaff thought. A lich soon. Instead he asked, "What do you think made him that way? Power?"

The elf rubbed a finger along the stem of her goblet while pondering the question. "He surrounds himself with mean little guards that want to hurt people. He was probably the same way as a kid. Tortured stray cats—you know—that kind of person."

Lysine, listening to the discussion leaned close to Higslaff. "Chaotic Black, is how I would classify him."

"Chaotic Black," Higslaff repeated. He knew that was a fancy way of saying the man was prone to random acts of evil. He knew that anyone who became so powerful was rarely so random in their acts. But they could be impulsive and self-centered.

"That is, of course," Lysine explained, "an observation based upon limited personal engagement."

Marigold interjected, "Who'd want to spend any personal time with that mean, wrinkled up old creep?"

The conversation veered away from the ancient magic user. Even when Higslaff steered it back, he learned little more than what his homunculus observed.

When the bard sat down for his first set of songs, he announced his first two were requests received earlier in the day. "First, *A Day in the Winterlands*," he said while plucking the strings to his ornate and highly polished psaltery, making sure all were in tune.

Higslaff's ears perked up. He motioned for everyone at the table to listen. "It's possible, this tale may shed some light on the old magic user." He glanced up at the questioning face of the tall elf. "Maybe why he's so mean."

"We heard another song about the Winterlands being attacked," Gurks said. "Happened about fifty, or a hundred years ago?"

"*Fall of the Winterlands*, "Higslaff said. "I'm guessing that could be the second request."

"Interesting," Lysine said.

Higslaff lifted his mug of beer. "Fortunate the God-Emperor's ambition didn't extend across the Narrowing Sea, to here."

"He's still alive?" the gnome healer asked.

Gurk replied, "Dude, what's fifty or a hundred years to someone everybody calls the God-Emperor?"

Then the clean-shaven bard announced, "One Day in the Winterlands."

Then he sang with a steady cadence:
A hundred hundred helms shone bright,
As the armies marched toward the fight,
Two hundred hundred feet marched on,
To meet the foe at Ebedon.

The walls before the army lay,
A small deterrent, perhaps a day.
They had marched long, they had marched far,
Under the banner of Ikasildar.

The defenders were few, but resolved to still stand,
As the last chance for saving the Winterland.
From Akbe to Blue Harbor, the cities lay cold,
Already defeated by the purple and gold.

The Aimen was dead, with Benemere and Roos,
They had faced death or slavery, and death they did choose.
Montremain had slain hundreds enjoying the kill,
Finally meeting his end when his sword had its fill.

Birdman and Patrick now wandered the planes,
As the Psionic Knights had dismantled their brains.
Mightyrenus had been vanquished at New Havnor,
Of the Zodiac, twelve had fallen, and there were no more.

Leviticus, the prophet, had returned at the last,
Though he could not survive the Bryaveir's blast.
The armies of both North and South were slain,
The rest fleeing to Vidkin with the merchant of Tanne.

So the last of the brave, the free and the true,
Watched the advancing armies—their fate they all knew.
To their gods and their patrons they lifted a prayer,
That they all would fight well with the Dragonslayer.

They knew from this battle few would still live,
And odds for their winning, the Gambling Monk wouldn't give.
So they faced their fate grimly, with their banners unfurled,
But to the last man they knew it was the end of the world.

After applause from those sitting at the benches in front of the stage, and the nearby tables, Marigold asked Higslaff, "What does that have to do with that creepy old magic user?"

"Like the Birdman, he's a refugee from the war," Lysine said.

The half-goblin thief shoved a piece of cheese in his mouth. "What do ya mean, dude?"

Lysine cleared his throat. "If I accurately recall, another song about the God-Emperor's conquest included the lines:

Telecarn, Cancer, Chi, and Sir Joshua too
Fought on like windstorms, and thousands they slew."

The druid looked at Higslaff with a questioning eyebrow. "Might you be suggesting 'Chi' is short for Chisisuschuherganteramoski?"

The pawnshop owner nodded affirmative.

"Then Chi and the Birdman are old comrades in arms," Kalgore said.

"Being a refugee for a hundred years," Marigold said. "That could make him mean. His home and everything taken by the God-Emperor."

"Maybe Chi was the one that fixed the Birdman's brain?" Jax said.

Higslaff flinched. He pressed his hand to his cheek and came away with blood.

"You are injured," the druid said. The adventuring party began scanning the room for the source of the pawnshop owner's wound.

Higslaff picked up a napkin and placed it over the deep cut. "Not to worry," he said, forcing a smile. "It stems from a dispute."

"Dude," the young thief said. "Someone's made a voodoo doll."

Higslaff dabbed the wound again. He had the Curing Elixir in his pocket, but didn't want to use it, yet. He dabbed again, trying not to flinch. "It will be settled tomorrow."

Jax extended his hand, reaching in front of the elf. "Give me your hand."

Higslaff knew the gnome was a healer, but shook his head, declining. "That's not necessary."

With remarkable dexterity, the elf snatched the bloody napkin with one hand and grabbed hold of the pawnshop owner's wrist with her other hand. Before he could pull back, she placed Higslaff's hand on the table. The gnome gripped it, and then Marigold leaned forward, pressing her breasts down over both hands.

"There," she said, still holding the pawnshop owner's arm in place. "Jax hates taking on pain when healing." She winked at Higslaff. "Call it positive reinforcement for him."

Kalgore said, "Never anything like that for me."

The elf rolled her eyes. "If I did, you'd get hurt on purpose."

"Maybe," the big warrior said, taking a bite of rye bread and showing a sly grin as he chewed.

The young thief laughed while the gnome muttered a spell.

The bard announced the requested song. "*Fall of the Winterlands.*"

"You're pretty smart," the young thief said to Higslaff.

While the song began the wound and its pain faded from Higslaff's cheek. It appeared on the gnome healer's face. The gnome flinched. Then, within seconds, the transferred wound began fading.

When the God-Emperor came down like a wolf on the fold
   And his cohorts were gleaming in purple and gold
   And the sheen of their spears was like the stars on the sea
   When the Kratzfians marched and laid siege to Akbe.

Like the leaves of the forest when summer is green
That host with their banners at sunset was seen.
Like the leaves of the forest when autumn has blown
Half the host on the morrow lay withered and strown.

Belagusta had aided with a fiery blast
And the Wizard of Winter felled more as he passed.
Montremain had slain generals with the Chaos Blade's charm
   And Meltarm had battled all who dared Justice harm.

But there stood defenders, eyes open, mouths wide,
   Through the ranks marched the God-Emperor, determined in stride.
   Belagusta challenged first, and was decimated unto smoke
   Then Archimedes, Mage of Ice Mountain, was the next to be broke.

   The mortals all stood, spirit broken and pale,
   'Till Benemere the White rode forth, in gleaming white mail.

The ranks were all silent as he battled alone.
He perished unheralded, with trumpets unblown.

The Kratzfians moved forward to press their advantage,
The defenders stood ready, courage as could manage.
The cresting attack took them over the walls
The fighting raged on, in doorways and in halls.

Telecarn, Cancer, Chi, and Sir Joshua too
Fought on like windstorms, and thousands they slew.
Aimen and Emperor battled near side by side.
Akbe was in crumble with nowhere to hide.

The pocks of resistance were being destroyed,
The fate of the Winterlands none could avoid.
Like Grahmlaug before, died defending his land,
Like the Hold of the Sea Princes, who'd failed to stand.

Covered in blood, crimson to the feet,
The Emperor of the South with sword raised, jeered defeat.
Ravaged his way to the embattled town square
Issued the God-Emperor to meet his end there.

Once again it halted, the bloody conquest
All eyes turn toward it, the despotic contest.
The defenders knew their last hope, their last gasp,
As a sun weary wanderer, one daring an asp.

Like fell darkness he came, came out of the night
Like cold blackness he struck, struck with all of his might.
Against such force, no mortal could stand
Even one so mighty, with the Chaos Sword in hand.

The Aimen knew this, and claiming his right
With Hammer of Justice, wagered into the fight.
The two battled on, relentless. The God-Emperor laughed.
Then laid them low with his strength and his craft.

The men of the Winterlands battled on, relentless, to the last.
The God-Emperor laid them low with his strength and his craft.

Marigold, lost in the song, forgot she'd been leaning forward. She sat back up straight.

Higslaff withdrew his wrist. "Thank you, Jax." He would've preferred not having his arm held by the gnome while it was pinned beneath the beautiful elf's more than ample bosom.

He reminded himself that she was a tease. He started to say something to Marigold, but she cut him off.

"No need to thank me too." She turned and rubbed the top of Jax's head. "I was just looking out for my friend."

Higslaff decided to let it drop. Clearly there was something about their relationship that he didn't want to know.

Beyond that, what the gnome healer, and what

Marigold did for him, wasn't asked for. He didn't want to give the impression that there was any form of debt or obligation. Besides, being stabbed in the face, over a distance, and trying to formulate a plan to deal with that powerful spellcaster left him detached, and unable to truly appreciate the elf's flirtiness. At any other time he would've responded differently. What man wouldn't?

It'd give him and Josiah something to discuss over a future lunch. He knew his friend was already jealous.

The bard began another song, this one about the unexpected, and ultimately tragic love a mountain giant had for a turquoise-haired mermaid.

Higslaff didn't really listen to the tale or the table's discussion that followed. He sipped his beer and tried to arrange what he knew about the ancient magic user and align those traits with other troublesome, and dangerous customers he'd dealt with.

Josiah noted his friend's distracted silence. He engaged Higslaff's guests, allowing his friend to maintain focus.

Very old, evil, highly skilled, knowledgeable, and accomplished in spellcraft—which didn't fit with impulsive. Egotistical, and a refugee—if not from Blue Harbor, then had probably spent time there. The last was an assumption, but from the little Higslaff read, Chisisuschugerganteramoski would've fit into the city's hierarchical structure.

The pawnshop owner finished his ale and suppressed a smile of satisfaction.

He knew what to offer for the exchange.

Chapter 23

Shortly after sunrise, Coleen Sammae arrived and cast her Ascertain Enchantment Spell, verifying that the adventuring party had indeed secured the Wand of Foe Detection.

Higslaff hadn't gotten much sleep, having to prepare the ransom item after departing the Blue Bugle. Why spend what might be all of his last hours sleeping? Several hours, so that he'd be on top of his negotiating game, was enough.

He secured the ransom item in a padded steel box. Sturdy but not fancy. That, he carried in a satchel.

The pawnshop owner climbed the steps to Josiah's barbershop and knocked on the door.

The muffled sound of the gray parrot saying, "Customer. Early customer," confirmed what he already knew. Josiah was awake.

The lay healer barber opened the door and let his friend in. The smell of mint tea and honey filled the shop.

"When are you to meet Sill Rochelle?" Josiah asked, heading to the back room to get the tea.

The shop was dark. The shutters remained closed, along with the door. Only a lantern lit the room. Higslaff sat down on one of the customer chairs.

"I have about fifteen minutes to spend with you, my friend. Then a brisk walk out of this unsavory neighborhood to her fancy gated and guarded apartment." Higslaff wasn't jealous. He expected an accomplished spellcaster to live in protective luxury.

Josiah returned with a tray bearing two cups of tea,

and two small plates with sliced bread and honey. Higslaff took his cup and plate. His friend knew how he preferred his tea and bread, and thanked him.

The two men ate and drank in silence. Helga flew down and got her small piece of bread, and a few grapes as well. The parrot was silent, which was odd for her.

Higslaff set his empty plate and cup on the chair next to him and pulled a leather scroll case from his satchel. "Wand's inside. Will you see that the guild gets it?"

Josiah, seated in his barber chair said, "I will do that."

The barber examined his friend. "Going armed with a mundane short sword?"

"The guards will disarm me before I go inside." Higslaff shrugged. "If not, I'll lose a fight no matter the sword I carry."

Josiah tipped his head from side to side, weighing the statement. "True, a fancy sword won't impress him."

Higslaff laughed grimly. "Why leave him a fancy gift?" He also carried a Healing Elixir and a Gem of Spell Absorption in his pocket. It was enchanted to negate one Mystic Missile Spell. Like many magic users and, as evidenced on the rat, that was probably Chi's "go to" spell to end an annoyance. It wouldn't alter the ultimate result if it came to a fight, but might allow Higslaff another moment to negotiate.

Josiah leaned forward in his chair and appraised his friend. "It's not required that you go."

"That's true, Josiah. It's not. But I think I have the negotiating edge in this one." The pawnshop owner got to his feet. "Thanks for the tea."

"Just angling." The barber stood and clasped his friend on the shoulder. "You did leave your shop to me in your will."

"Ha! Like Black Venom would allow *that* to happen." Both men recognized the joke. Handing such a business off to a blood relative would be acceptable—if he had one ready.

"Lunch here tomorrow?" the barber asked.

"Yep." Higslaff headed for the door. "Your turn to buy."

Sill Rochelle was both prim and grim, with narrow eyes and lips. She preferred faded blue and grays. Her heavy cotton blouse and wool dress reflected that.

As she led Higslaff around to the small, secluded flower garden beneath her apartment's window, Higslaff said, "You know, it's midsummer." He gestured at her outfit.

"Do I comment on your ridiculous hat collection—all the same style?"

"Actually, at least once a month."

She took in a deep breath, enjoying the fragrance of her yellow and orange day lilies, and climbing purple and pink morning glories. "Then I shall strive to double that frequency."

He pulled the leather case containing a Transport scroll from his satchel and handed it to her. He'd already given her the substantial coin for her services.

She carefully placed the scroll case in her own satchel. "Are you prepared?"

After Higslaff nodded, she took his hand and began

her spell.

Higslaff hated the way Transport Spells made his ears pop. Besides the cost, another reason he rarely had one cast upon him. He shook his head and looked around. They were in an apple orchard, just off the main road, a half mile from Shorn Spearhead.

They approached the city together, in silence. Sill Rochelle wasn't a great conversationalist, but they often talked shop. Today Higslaff had too many thoughts running through his head to carry the conversation. Instead he mentally rehearsed phrasing and potential branches the negotiation might take.

After they walked through the main gate, Sill Rochelle said, "I shall be at the Aviary Inn. If you do not contact me there by midmorning tomorrow, I shall depart."

That was their agreement. She was experienced and professional enough not to ask for any details.

"Hopefully, we can return before then." He glanced at the sun, risen at least an hour. "Maybe noon, with any luck."

Sill Rochelle must've recognized that Higslaff's business offered risk to his health, or worse, because she said, "I hope you do have luck. I'd be pleased for you to share a late lunch at the Crow's Gullet with me."

Higslaff smiled. Subconsciously he rested a hand on his sword's pommel. "I'll see what I can do to make that happen, Sill."

Chapter 24

"Turn around," the half-goblin guard said. "Only business you've got here is if you're looking to die."

Higslaff could see in the two guards' eyes that they had no qualms about killing. While those types could bring trouble from authorities, they generally were the most effective type of guards.

The path up to the apartment door was short and narrow. One guard had his hand on his scimitar's grip and the other had nocked an arrow and began to draw it back.

Higslaff said, "The magic user within requested my presence."

"Your name?"

Higslaff maintained a relaxed stance with his sword hand gripping the satchel's leather strap. "He'll know me as Higslaff, the pawnshop owner."

The guard with the scimitar signaled for his partner to check. The other guard lowered his bow and knocked twice on the thick wooden door.

Higslaff suspected they were in for a long wait. After only a minute the door cracked open. The bow-wielding guard relayed that Higslaff the Pawnshop Owner was there to see the boss.

The door closed, and the two guards returned to their "ready to attack" stance.

"Might I make two suggestions, that'll improve your already effectiveness at warding your boss's residence. And make your job easier?"

"Ha!" The scimitar wielding goblin drew his weapon and sneered. "What does a pawnshop owner know about guarding important men?"

"Hear me out, sirs." Higslaff stood his ground. "If what I suggest makes sense, you can benefit from it. If not, what have you lost by listening?"

The second guard raised his bow and drew back the arrow further. "I'll have lost peace and quiet listening to your garbage." He showed his pointed teeth in a snarling grin. "I'd rather listen to you squeal with my arrow in your gut."

"Your boss may enjoy that sound too." Higslaff shrugged. "Then again, since he requested my presence, maybe not." It was possible the magic user had a familiar listening. Chisisuschugerganteramoski might even be seated near one of the apartment's shuttered windows himself. On the off chance he was overheard, sounding relaxed, confident, and willing to offer sound professional advice could only help.

A quiet moment passed. Higslaff watched a large grackle with iridescent head feathers land and snap up a small insect beneath a nearby thorny bush.

The guards eventually lowered their weapons.

"What's your idea for making our job easier?" the scimitar guard asked.

"Only two things." He gestured toward the scimitar. "Get a spear to go with your scimitar. Point it at people like me when they approach. More intimidating having the sharp point angled at their heart, or face. Makes them keep their distance, and will give your partner a better chance of shooting, should the individual be so foolish as to close.

"Gives you something to throw at troublemakers, besides insults. Lean it against the wall until you need it."

The scimitar guard curled his lip, but didn't dismiss

the suggestion.

"You said, two." The other guard sneered. "What about me?"

Higslaff said, "Get a crossbow, with a goat's foot lever. It appears that you have to wait before guests are admitted. Easier to hold a crossbow on a man.

"Doesn't have to be big or too strong of a draw, since you don't have far to shoot. The close-quarters accuracy and mechanics of a crossbow are more intimidating."

The half-goblin lifted his bow and drew back, pointing the nocked arrow at Higslaff's face. "You sayin' I ain't intimidating?"

"I said *more* intimidating."

Higslaff glanced back at the scimitar guard. "Spent my share of years standing guard. Clerics and merchants. Never fortunate enough for magic users."

The scimitar guard grunted. The bow guard lowered his arrow's aim.

The door behind the guards cracked open. "The boss'll see him."

The scimitar guard said, "Gimme your sword."

Higslaff pulled it from the scabbard. He handed it grip first to the guard and stepped through the threshold, following the third half-goblin guard.

The apartment's entry room was dark and unadorned, as was the hallway leading to the ancient magic user's study. No art or furniture, or even a rug. It was possible the magic user didn't value such things. If so, that was troubling for Higslaff's plan. It might also reflect the man had just moved in, or didn't intend to stay. Or he lacked sufficient coin.

Shorn Spearhead wasn't a large town, and the number of residences suitable to a powerful individual were limited. New arrival and temporary accommodations would be the assumption he'd work under. Of course, evil and cruel individuals sometimes shunned art and nature's beauty. That sort of shunning eliminated a third of his ransom item's appeal.

The last possibility, lack of coin didn't fit. Powerful magic users, even ones prone to gambling debts, could always secure coin. And this man had guards. They were not elite. Nor were they incompetent.

A weak Light Spell lit the narrow hallway. They passed one door on the right on the way to the one at the end of the hallway. The guard knocked twice, waited several seconds, and then opened the door a crack.

"Admit the merchant."

Chisisuschugerganteramoski's voice was dry with age, but carried strength and self-assurance.

Sunlight filtering through two narrow windows lit the small study. Chisisuschugerganteramoski sat at a table facing away from the door. The guard led Higslaff around to stand between the table and the windows. A flick of the ancient magic user's age-spotted hand dismissed the half-goblin guard.

Before the door closed the magic user, who hadn't lifted his head from reading a large, leather-bound tome, said, "Tell the maid to prepare a cup of hot tea. Have it to me in five minutes."

Higslaff shrugged to himself. A less than subtle signal that he didn't merit much time. It was better than being wounded through his homunculus, which he'd been expecting. Less predictable than Higslaff hoped for.

Besides the book on the table, on the end to the magic user's left, rested the cage. A folded tablecloth covered it. Even this close, Higslaff couldn't sense his homunculus's presence. The enchanted creature might smell his master. A magical cage that barred sense of smell didn't seem necessary. Depriving humans of light for sight, sounds to hear, and smells for days and weeks was a form of coercion his guild used. But that wouldn't work on an enchanted creature like a homunculus. Their brains were different, just like their needs and desires.

Higslaff stood quietly, taking in the contents of the sparse room while the magic user ran a finger across the text that covered a page in the book. It was part of the negotiation game. Usually, however, it was he who made people wait. It sparked a bit of anger, but he quickly doused it. He needed to keep a clear head. Not show any anger or frustration.

The ancient magic user eventually looked up. "Merchant, you are here to regain control of your homunculus." From beneath his robes, the magic user lifted a dagger and placed it on the table. "You have until my tea arrives, or neither of you will leave this room."

Higslaff believed any servant working for this man would be prompt, so he had fewer than two minutes. He reached into his satchel and withdrew the box. "May I place what I have brought to exchange for my homunculus on your table?"

When the ancient magic user didn't reply one way or the other, Higslaff proceeded. He opened the box and placed the item on the table. It was a bottle carved from rare blue quartz crystal to resemble a stalagmite.

Higslaff saw a slight size increase in the ancient magic user's pupils. He witnessed the same when poker players drew a favorable hand.

"The crystal bottle is from the now destroyed palace in Blue Harbor. It contained perfume used by Emperor

Xaggcer's eldest daughter." Higslaff shrugged. "That is what I was told, however, I do not believe its origin can be traced that precisely.

"It no longer holds perfume. It contains a Minor Elixir of Summers."

"You disturb my study, to offer a perfume vial holding a potion that will return two to seven summers to the one that imbibes it?" Indignation and impatience filled his voice.

A breath later the magic user completed a spell. A flurry of brown Mystic Missiles flew from his pointed finger and into the pawnshop owner.

They veered slightly from their intended point of impact, and instead struck into Higslaff's shirt pocket, where he'd placed his Gem of Mystic Missile Absorption. The abruptness and magnitude of the spell attack caught Higslaff off guard. He stepped back, almost losing his balance. He managed to steady himself against the wall behind him.

The spell's failure didn't appear to fluster the powerful magic user. He reached over and pulled the cloth from atop the cage. "Your familiar is not adorned with enchanted trinkets."

Higslaff gathered his courage, and kept his voice even. "Am I to take it you've reneged upon your promise that I had until your tea arrived?"

Chisisuschugerganteramoski picked up his dagger and said, "Your offer was made, and rejected."

"I was not finished." Higslaff returned to where he'd been standing.

The ancient magic user shoved the dagger's tip into the cage, drawing blood from both Snix's and Higslaff's leg. "Finish, then. But be quick." He stabbed the same leg a second time.

The homunculus hissed and showed his teeth. Higslaff bit his lower lip and leaned on his good, right leg.

"You are new to the region," Higslaff said, keeping his voice level, almost monotone. "If you are simply passing through, the results of this negotiation and my fate will be unimportant to you. However, if you intend to establish yourself, then what happens in the next minute will have long-term repercussions."

The magic user laughed a dry cackle. "You threaten me?"

"I do not." Higslaff reached down and felt the blood on his thigh. "You threaten your ability to establish trust and agreements for years to come." He struggled to keep his voice even. "You are skilled, powerful and knowledgeable. The most powerful spellcaster I have met face to face. For right or wrong, if word were to get out that you're an unreliable client, those with connections, and access to resources you desire—"

"And I suppose you are a person with connections and resources I desire."

Rather than wasting what time he had left, debating that point, Higslaff said, "You could certainly summon enchanted creatures far more fierce, impressive and effective as guards than those you've hired. Although you could, your energy and resources are better spent, and those you've hired suffice.

"If you were to mistreat or slay those guards, recruiting replacements would be more difficult, and more costly."

The ancient magic user cut in, saying, "And your death, merchant, will cost me coin, and tarnish my reputation." His dry cackle returned. "What is one more twig cast into a furnace?"

"If it's a new fire, one twig at a strategic moment may affect the course of the furnace's flame." It wasn't a great analogy but, under the circumstances, it best Higslaff could come up with.

There was a knock at the door. After a few seconds, an elderly woman with gray hair tied up in a bun entered. She may have been attractive in her youth. She wore a gray, sackcloth dress and carried a small steaming pot of tea along with a cup and saucer on a tray. As if she'd completed the task a thousand times, she pulled a tall table from its place against the wall to within the magic user's reach. She set the tray and its contents on the table without making eye contact.

After pouring a partial cup, she lifted it to her lips and drank. Without a word or facial expression, she poured a full cup and departed the room, pulling the door closed behind her.

Higslaff waited, as did Snix. Higslaff was pretty sure the magic user wouldn't use fire, or lightning. But another Mystic Missile or a myriad of other spells, such as Crystal Encasement, could do him in.

The magic user drank his tea and stared at the blue crystal bottle.

The old magic user sat down his empty cup and picked up his dagger. "Tell me, merchant, where did you get the crystal vial and the elixir?"

"I own a pawnshop, in Three Hills City. From my inventory. The crystal was pawned by a young noblewoman. She did not pay for its return within the allotted time. The elixir, traded for from an elf warrior."

"Are you so driven by coin that you didn't drink it

yourself?"

Higslaff gave the honest answer. "The elven adventurer sold it to me over a decade ago. If I still had it when it came time to retire, I planned on drinking it."

"So you can extend your life as a merchant."

"No. So that I could relive those years with some health, doing something else."

The ancient magic user laughed. "You're lying. If not to me, then to yourself."

Maybe Chisisuschugerganteramoski was right. His shop was his life. "You asked, and I told you my plan. The vial and the elixir it holds are yours now."

A mischievous look crossed the ancient magic user's face. It was a disturbing look.

"I shall see that the elixir is added to the drink on the wedding night of one of a newly wedded couple. The husband's cup, I think." The ancient magic user grinned, showing perfectly strait, white teeth. "With luck, it will ruin that evening, and many to come."

That seemed like a spiteful, if not trifling use. There must be a reason the magic user wouldn't drink it himself, but it wasn't Higslaff's place to ask. He could be lying, or trying to be humorous. All Higslaff cared about was that the magic user had plans for the elixir. It could mean he'd accepted it in trade, and Higslaff might see another day.

"I am preparing to build a new residence," Chisisuschugerganteramoski said. "Do you have anything else from Blue Harbor? Furniture, paintings?" He gestured toward the blue quartz crystal bottle. "Sculptures?"

"I have a single saucer for a tea service bearing a picture of Emperor Montremain wielding the Chaos

Sword. The quality is far less than exceptional." He held forward his hand. "If we are working towards an equitable exchange, for my homunculus, and my life, I would like to use the Minor Elixir of Curing, I also brought."

Chisisuschugerganteramoski seemed to notice, for the first time, the blood seeping from the wound, staining the pawnshop owner's pants. "No."

Higslaff wasn't surprised by the answer. He nodded and continued. "Items from Blue Harbor, especially the destroyed palace, are difficult to come by. With effort, and some luck, I could secure some for you. Delivery to Shorn Spearhead would be easy to arrange."

The magic user shook his head. "The Dark Heart Swamp. I have laid claim to an abandoned outpost shrine of Hades."

"The Dark Heart Swamp," Higslaff said, no enthusiasm in his voice. "Goblins, lizard men." He shook his head, and made eye contact with the old wizard. "There's a dragon and a lich that also live in the swamp."

"The dragon's lair is far to the north. Malthia the Cursed is consumed with finding some enchanted item. By the time she turns her attention to me, I shall be established. Challenging me then will prove the end of her existence."

That sounded overly self-assured to Higslaff, especially when facing the wrath of a lich. None of his business. He knew he wasn't out of danger yet. Chisisuschugerganteramoski's mind could change in an instant. If he'd even guessed the malicious cruelty of the magic user, Higslaff wouldn't have sought his homunculus's release. The adventuring party had been lucky to secure his services without somehow suffering.

Possibly Marigold's beauty and charm carried more influence than she thought?

Higslaff settled on demonstrating knowledge to further his cause. "I have heard of the outpost you've claimed. My understanding is that the lich recently searched the water-filled dungeon. She will be familiar with the layout of your claim."

The ancient magic user's wispy eyebrows rose briefly. He brought his index finger to his lips and tapped. "Are you certain of Malthia's search of my outpost?"

"As certain as one can be about a lich's actions." He held his hands out, palms up. "An adventuring party talked about seeing the lich leading a band of goblins that direction. And I heard tell from a source within the Church of Apollo about the exploring of the Hades outpost."

"Higslaff, you are more than a merchant."

"I'm competent with a sword. Knowledge about things of value and common enchanted items are important to running a successful pawnshop. I've learned and heard a lot along the way, and still do."

"Take your homunculus and don't cross me again, merchant." The last word uttered dripped sarcasm. He unlocked the cage and knocked it to the floor.

Snix scrambled out of the cage and up his master's good leg, and climbed to perch on his shoulder.

"Verify or disprove Malthia's visit to my claim in the swamp, and anyone else who'd visited it." He poured himself a second cup of tea and pulled the shawl tight around his shoulders. "Use your connections to find art and relics from Blue Harbor.

"I'll visit your pawnshop in Three Hills City in the

fall. You'll tell me what you learned. If I like the art and relics you've gathered, I'll pay fair coin and arrange for delivery."

Higslaff tipped his head and smiled, trying to ignore the pain in his leg. "I look forward to it."

Chisisuschugerganteramoski pointed a crooked finger at the pawnshop owner. "Don't lie to me, merchant." With a remarkably steady hand for someone so old, he sipped his tea. "No one looks forward to a visit from me."

EPILOGUE

In a cellar connected to the tunnel system beneath Three Hills City

Hallum lay on his side, his hands bound behind his back, his legs tied with leather cords at the knees and ankles. A wad of cloth soaked full with his saliva filled his mouth, making it impossible to speak or spit the mass out.

The flame of a lantern hanging on a wall hook flickered, creating shadows on the damp walls. Although the wick was set low, the illumination clearly outlined the dwarf guard standing erect and alert against the opposite wall, near the room's only door.

For the ten-thousandth time Hallum cursed Daxel for Transporting away in the middle of the fight—one they were winning. Cursed Daxel for abandoning him for no reason, other than cowardice.

Hallum had no illusions about what awaited him. Torture, until he divulged information. Something he knew well—but not from the receiving end. He wondered if such knowledge would help him endure, or magnify each pain and horror inflicted.

Without a knock or any other warning, the ill-fitted door swung open. A lean man with a long face and broad shoulders strode in, his boots making no sound on the pea gravel floor. He wore a black shirt with a black leather vest, pants and boots, which accentuated his pale face and hands. His thin mustache, goatee beard, and shoulder-length straight black hair furthered the effect.

A second man followed him into the cellar. His clothes were ragged and torn and his skin was a mottled gray. It was a zombie. Hallum recognized the corpse. He'd been a fellow guild member named Paulter. He was last seen outside a tavern in Riven Rock a month ago. Why nobody'd seen him since was now obvious.

A cold shiver ran down Hallum's spine as he recognized his fate. The shivering spread to his bound limbs, like he'd just been pulled from beneath a frozen river.

The pale man pointed to Hallum and asked, "Do you recognize this man?" The voice was deep, cold and distant, like he didn't care what the answer was.

The zombie, who had once been Paulter answered. "I do." The voice lacked emotion. It sounded like hollow exhaustion.

That the zombie spoke shocked Hallum so much that he stopped shivering. Paulter's undead corpse held a spark of life—intelligence in his eyes. His eyes also held sadness.

"Will he have information of value to me?"

"He will."

Hallum heard Paulter's voice in the words, spoken as if through a hollow log filled with sopping wet moss.

He sounded empty, and beaten.

The pale-skinned man stepped forward, reached down and lifted Hallum by the front of his shirt as if he were a child. The pale man opened his mouth, revealing fangs.

Further dread fell upon Hallum's heart, like frozen lead. It was Black Venom, the enemy guild's leader. The captured thief struggled like a worm caught on a fish hook, to no avail. Sharp fangs sank into his neck.

As the Three Hills City's guild master drank his blood,

Hallum felt strength drain from his muscles. His body grew cold.

After the vampire dropped his meal, he said to the dwarf, "Kill him. Painful, but fast, then get the corpse to Galthorn."

The vampire placed the tip of his boot beneath Hallum's chin and lifted it. "The value of what you know lessens with time. But, not to worry. You'll join your guild friend…" He glanced over at the dwarf.

Answering the unspoken question, the dwarf said. "I believe Paulter was his name."

"Ahh, Paulter," Black Venom said to the dwarf, and nodded approval. He then shifted his body and turned his head while keeping his boot's toe unmoving beneath Hallum's chin. He asked the zombie, "Was your name Paulter?"

The zombie replied tonelessly, "Yes."

"Inside your undead body, are you still Paulter?"

"Yes."

"Tell me, Paulter. What do you think of your existence as a souled zombie?"

"Miserable."

Despite the dreary weakness permeating every muscle, Hallum began to shake uncontrollably again. The only warmth he felt came from the trickle of urine wetting his trousers.

"Yes, a quick, painful death." The vampire stared down at the terrified man. He pulled back his boot, letting Hallum's chin drop into the pea gravel. He said to the dwarf, "After Galthorn animates his corpse, with soul intact, and he tells us all we want to know…"

The vampire turned to the animated corpse standing two steps behind him. "Zombie, what is that man's name?"

"Hallum."

Hallum looked up at Paulter, then to Black Venom. He tried to cry out, "No, please, I'll tell you anything," but the gag holding the wad of saliva-soaked cloth in his mouth muffled the desperate words.

Black Venom turned back to the dwarf. "Remind the animated corpse that was Hallum that it can look forward to decades of misery. Misery earned through imprudent choices."

The End

About the Author

Terry W. Ervin II is an English teacher who enjoys writing fantasy and science fiction.

Pawn is the fifth book in Terry's *Monsters, Maces and Magic* series (LitRPG fantasy). He is the author of two other series: *Crax War Chronicles* (science fiction) and the *First Civilization's Legacy Series* (fantasy). Terry has also written a post-apocalyptic alien invasion novel titled **Thunder Wells**, and a short story collection, **Genre Shotgun**. Finally, Terry co-authored **Cavern**, a *Dane Maddock Adventure*, with author David Wood.

When Terry isn't writing or enjoying time with his wife and daughters, he can be found in his basement raising turtles.

To contact Terry, or to learn more about his writing endeavors, visit his website at www.ervin-author.com and his blog, *Up Around the Corner*.

Made in the USA
Monee, IL
13 October 2020